VISION SINISTER

Could two young women look through a slide in a door and see a girl being murdered — and yet find the room beyond completely empty when they come to enter it with the police? Dr Hiram Carruthers, the famous back-room physicist and investigator, together with Chief Inspector Garth of Scotland Yard, sets out on a tortuous trail. Though the mystery of the killer's identity is not for long in doubt, the method used is a puzzle — until the cynical master-scientist Carruthers fits the pieces into place.

JOHN RUSSELL FEARN

VISION SINISTER

Complete and Unabridged

LINFORD
Leicester

First published in Great Britain in 1954

First Linford Edition
published 2005

British Library CIP Data

Fearn, John Russell, *1908 – 1960*
    Vision sinister.—Large print ed.—
    Linford mystery library
    1. Detective and mystery stories
    2. Large type books
    I. Title
    823.9'12 [F]

    ISBN 1–84395–749–3

Published by
F. A. Thorpe (Publishing)
Anstey, Leicestershire

Set by Words & Graphics Ltd.
Anstey, Leicestershire
Printed and bound in Great Britain by
T. J. International Ltd., Padstow, Cornwall

This book is printed on acid-free paper

1

'I suppose it's ridiculous to feel nervous, particularly when you're going to meet your fiancé — but there it is. It isn't *Terry* I'm afraid of, of course, only the basement he's taken over for his experimental work.'

Cynthia Harwood gave a nervous little smile, yet it had withal a hopeful quality. She was a dark, good-looking girl of twenty-five, debarred from complete serenity of expression by the sharpness of her chin. Here was a girl with determination, yet perhaps not too much of it to spoil her femininity.

'And so, being scared to death, you want me to come with you?'

'As my best friend, yes. Two girls are better than one, after all, and I can hardly visit my fiancé with another *man* in tow.'

'Hardly,' Janice Worthing smiled — as blonde as Cynthia was dark. 'And naturally I'll come. I'd rather like to meet

1

the boy friend. He sounds a frightfully mysterious sort of person.'

'Not really, he isn't: there couldn't be a more open boy anywhere. Only I'm a bit bothered about this place he's taken over. It's a basement at — er — ' Cynthia opened her handbag and consulted a square of paper. 'At forty-two, Andmouth Street. That's in the East End and about thirty minutes from here. His main hobby is photography, both movie and still, and he needed a good dark-room. Hence the basement. Anyway, he rang me up this morning and said would I call and see his new laboratory tonight, so there it is. He thinks nothing of being in a dubious quarter in a basement but *I* do. I'll feel a hundred per cent safer with you beside me.'

Janice glanced towards the mantle-clock. 'Did he give any particular time?'

'He said seven-thirty, and since it's pitch dark at that time I don't feel like a lone exploration of Andmouth Street.'

'Naturally you don't . . . ' Janice's brows knitted as she pursued an inner thought and Cynthia glanced at her enquiringly.

'Something bothering you?'

'No, not really. I was just thinking it's rather strange that *he* didn't call for *you* and take you to his basement. George would have done that for me.'

'George and Terry have no similarity,' Cynthia sighed. 'Terry is so completely casual about everything it probably never occurred to him to act as my escort. It isn't that he's deliberately discourteous. He just doesn't even think of such things.'

Janice shrugged. 'Oh well, if that's the way you like 'em, its no affair of mine. And since it's quarter to seven now we'd better be on our way. I'll just get my things.'

'See you in the car then,' Cynthia said, rising. 'It's parked in the Crescent.'

And within ten minutes the two girls were on their way, Cynthia at the wheel of her trim little two-seater. With Cynthia money was not a consideration. She was a commercial artist of very high standing, possessed of unique gifts when it came to artistic advertising, and because of this very uniqueness, money came easily — and went easily, too. With Janice it was a different matter. She had no particular gifts that she knew of, unless they lay in her ability to be a devoted wife and home-maker. To her, George Worthing — whom she had married six months before — was the be-all and end-all of her little sphere. Not for her the worldly outlook and sophistication of Cynthia.

And herein, for Janice, there lay something of a puzzle. Why should Cynthia, usually so calmly efficient and ready to do battle with the world, be so scared of visiting a basement laboratory used by her husband-to-be? The only possible reason that Janice could think of was natural feminine fear. Yes, that must be it.

Well within the half-hour Cynthia had negotiated the main hub of brightly lighted London, and her car finally nosed its way into the drear regions wherein lay Andmouth Street. It proved to be fairly close to the dock area — a dismal neighbourhood of fitfully winking gaslights and damply gleaming pavements.

Janice gave a little shiver as she peered

around her through the car's steamed windows.

'Now I can understand why you wanted company! What on earth your boy friend was thinking of to come into a dump like this, I can't imagine! Couldn't he find somewhere in a better neighbourhood?'

'He said he couldn't. Anyway, we'd better start walking.'

Cynthia drew the car to a stop and slid out into the spasmodic glimmerings of the lamplight. Janice followed her, then with the car doors locked, they started walking slowly, half fearfully, indeed, wishing the high heels of their shoes did not make such a noise. Any moment they expected some undesirable to loom out of the fine, chilling mist.

'Far as I know,' Cynthia said after a moment, 'Andmouth Street is one of these on the left here.'

Such proved to be the case. Andmouth Street was a cul-de-sac with a high wall at the far end, beyond which were the green, red, and amber lights of a goods sidings. To either side of the street the two girls beheld the towering, unlovely façades of small factories, warehouses, and granaries evidently connected with the docks.

Nowhere a sign of anybody as the two girls walked slowly along the gloomy vista. They were constantly on the watch for trouble, but nothing showed itself, and after a while Cynthia started to count off the numbers of the buildings.

'Thirty-six — thirty-eight — forty . . . That must be forty-two past that bit of waste land there. Looks like an old theatre or cinema, or something.'

Janice nodded in the dim light, surveying the tall, leprous structure which was evidently number forty-two. The gable end which overlooked the waste stretch was defaced by a long, obliterated hoarding, a quarter of it flapping idly in the wet, chilly wind. The front of the building had the same forlorn look, yet there was definitely something about it that stamped it as a one-time theatre, music hall, or some kind of entertainment establishment.

'Are you sure Terry wasn't pulling your leg?' Janice asked dubiously, as they paused and surveyed the old edifice. 'From the look of things I'd say this place is just derelict.'

'Building itself is, certainly, but that doesn't stop the basements being used for trade purposes, I suppose. Let's see what we can find.'

As curious as a couple of schoolgirls they wandered round the side of the great deserted place, the lamplights casting sufficient illumination for their now accustomed eyes to see fairly clearly. So it was they came presently to what looked like glowing squares set in the concrete stretch on the inner side of the pavement.

'There you are!' Cynthia exclaimed in delight. 'There *are* basements below. And lights, too! Only problem is how to get to them . . .'

It did not remain a problem for long, for at the rear of the building there lay a cindered area that had been — and perhaps still was — a car park. At the further end of it was a small illuminated sign with an arrow pointing downwards. It said quite distinctly: *Commercial Basements*.

'There we are!' Cynthia exclaimed in relief. 'The only explanation is that the building itself is derelict but the basements are used for commercial purposes. Come on . . . '

They hurried across the cindered area and so arrived at a flight of quite modern imitation granite steps leading downwards to an area of bright light. Everything was quite clean and hygienic — the walls tiled and the lights of quite up-to-date electric variety — and at the base of the steps a fairly narrow tunnel stretched away into distance.

'I get it,' Janice exclaimed abruptly. 'This is, perhaps, part of an old Underground system, converted to commercial use.'

'Could be,' Cynthia assented. 'Certainly not so spooky now as I'd expected.'

They came presently to the first of many doors. It sported a rather gay enamelled sign that read: *Cute Lips Cosmetics*. The next door further on belonged to Kingfisher Chemical Company, and indeed all the doors, as the girls passed them, bore quite normal commercial signs, so evidently all was in order in spite of the somewhat nerve-tingling approach.

'Ah!' Cynthia exclaimed abruptly, halting, 'Here we are!'

Janice paused, too, and together they surveyed a door which had a small plate screwed to it. It said: *Terence Hewlett, Photographer. Dark Room. Please look through Inspection Shutter and if Red Light is On there will be delay in answering door.*

'Sounds fair enough,' Janice commented. 'I suppose that is the inspection shutter.'

She nodded to a small eye-width slide set in the door at standing level. To it was affixed a rounded knob.

'That'll be it,' Cynthia assented. 'Looks like one of those things they use in gangster films. You know, where an ugly mug looks through before letting you in.'

'It does at that. Only difference there is that the slide is worked from the inside, and this is worked from the outside. Well, push it aside and let's have a look.'

'I'll ring first,' Cynthia decided, and pressed the button on the side of the door.

There was no sound of the bell ringing beyond, unless the door was perhaps very thick and virtually sound-proof. Nor did anybody attempt to answer the summons. So Cynthia reached before her and drew the glide gently back, peering through it into the space beyond.

'Great — great heavens!' she whispered at length, and the odd tone of her voice made Janice glance at her sharply.

'What is it? Something wrong?'

As Cynthia did not respond but remained staring through the slide fixedly, curiosity got the better of Janice's manners. Since only one of them could see through the narrow slide at a time, she elbowed Cynthia out of the way and looked for herself — to become as horribly fascinated as Cynthia had been.

She was looking straight into a rather dimly lighted laboratory, or else a dark room. She could distinctly see a heavy bench loaded with all manner of jars and equipment. In the background was a big photographic enlarger and at closer quarters a large movie projector of the professional type. Overhead was a lamp casting a pinkish white glow downwards upon a most amazing scene.

There was a girl, slim and mid-blonde, in evening dress. She half lay across a heavy table, her arms straining with all their power against the strength of the white-overalled man towering over her. In one hand he held a glittering knife, and upon his face there was an expression of frozen ferocity.

So much Janice realised — then the knife suddenly descended. The girl quivered spasmodically, her arms became flaccid and dropped helplessly. Her entire body slithered from the insecure support of the table and collapsed on the floor.

Janice screamed. It was the only reaction of which she was capable. She screamed as loudly as she possibly could and then stumbled back from the door slide. Cynthia stared within for a few brief seconds, her face drawn with strain, then she slammed the slide back into place and stood breathing hard.

'Murder!' Janice panted, staring at her. 'He killed her! I saw him do it — '

'Yes. Yes, I know.' Cynthia seemed to be trying desperately to think. 'It's Terry in there all right. I don't know the girl at all — You saw him? Saw his face?'

'Course I did!' Janice's eyes were staring. 'What do we *do*?'

'He's got to explain himself!' Cynthia snapped, and jabbed the bell-push firmly.

There was no response. Evidently Terry was not taking any chances. Janice reached out to the slide, but Cynthia stopped her.

'Never mind that now. Terry or otherwise, we've got to get the police . . . We've *got* to, Janice!'

'Anything wrong here, ladies?'

The girls turned sharply. They had been so absorbed in what they must do next that they had not heard the approach of a man in overalls. From his age and general appearance, together with his smouldering briar, they judged he must be the caretaker.

'Are you in charge of these basement

offices and work-rooms?' Cynthia asked quickly.

'That's right, lady. Anything happened? I thought I 'eard somebody scream. Sounded like a woman — '

'I screamed,' Janice said, on the edge of hysteria. 'I — I saw something horrible. In this laboratory here! A man murdering a girl ... They're in there now!'

'What!' The caretaker stared, his eyes very round.

'It's right enough,' Cynthia confirmed, steadying herself. 'The man concerned is my fiancé Mr. Hewlett. Whether that be so or not he's murdered or gravely injured a girl in that laboratory of his — You'd better fetch a policeman, fast as you can.'

'Aye! I will that!' And the caretaker raced away quickly down the long passage, leaving the two girls looking after him.

Abruptly Janice turned to the nearby door and again whipped back the slide and peered through it. This time there was nothing visible, only the dim reflection of her own eyes and part of her face. Slowly she re-closed the slide.

'Well?' Cynthia asked, set-faced and troubled.

'He's put out the light. He must be hiding there in the dark. You'd wonder he wouldn't try to get out quickly.'

'Knowing we've been ringing? Hardly! He's probably waiting until he thinks we've gone away.'

'Think he knows we saw him?'

'He may do — but I doubt it. He was too intent on — on his villainy to notice much else.'

Janice nodded slowly and then began to move around in agitated little steps, a nervous reaction which she maintained until at length there were echoing footsteps down the long, tiled tunnel, and the caretaker reappeared, the massive figure of a constable coming up behind him.

'Now, ladies, what's all this about?' The constable had a solidity and quiet respect about him that was immensely heartening. 'The caretaker here says . . . murder.'

'I think it is that, yes.' Cynthia tried to

sound calm — and then she explained in detail. The constable listened, made a note or two, and finally turned to the caretaker.

'You'll have a key for this laboratory, or whatever it is, I suppose?'

'Yes, I've got duplicates of all the basements along 'ere. Wait a minute while I get 'em.'

The caretaker was only gone a few moments and returned with a small split steel hoop on which were a variety of keys. After an exasperating delay due to myopia and no glasses he finally found the right one and wriggled it into the door lock. Pulling the key free again he pushed the door wide and reached beyond.

'I'll do that,' the constable said curtly. 'Get behind me, all of you. This may be dangerous.'

The switch clicked under his groping hand, and light from a hundred-watt lamp at the end of a single flex came into being. Only . . . Only the laboratory was not there any more. There *was* *no* *laboratory*. Nothing, except a perfectly empty basement about twelve by fifteen feet, its furthest slightly circular wall and the square walls to either side all cleanly white with new distemper. The concrete floor was tidy and had no dust upon it. On the doorward wall was an unexciting 15-amp plug.

The constable turned very slowly, his beefy face one of dark suspicion.

'This intended as some kind of a joke?' he asked heavily. 'Doesn't do to play tricks like this, you know. Makes me think I was called away from my beat whilst a robbery or something could be committed!'

'But — but this is beyond understanding!' Janice was staring stupidly about her upon the immaculate walls.

'We saw a murder being committed in here! Not only that — there were fixtures, like a bench, with dozens of bottles. Then there was a heavy table with a girl lying across it, and . . . and . . . '

Janice's voice trailed off, a not surprising thing considering the cold suspicion of the constable's stare.

'I can only think,' he said at length,

'that you two young ladies are playing some kind of a joke. There's certainly nothing here: you can see that for yourselves.'

He made a sweeping gesture that would have done credit to any dramatic actor, and the movement of his arm took in the newly distempered walls and the barrenness in all directions. There was no doubt about it. There was nothing — absolutely nothing — in the basement.

Struck with a sudden thought, Cynthia turned quickly to the door and examined it, particularly the slide through which she and Janice had both seen the tragedy enacted. There was nothing wrong here, either. Clear glass was embedded in the slot, and the wooden slide itself was, of course, on the outer side of the door.

'I'm wasting time here,' the constable said gruffly. 'I'll not book you this time, ladies, but I'm giving you a warning. Any more nonsense like this and there'll be trouble.'

He turned impatiently to leave, but Cynthia barred the way.

'Just a moment, constable . . . ' Her face was pale but earnest as she looked up at him. 'What we saw through this door really happened! One of us could have been mistaken I suppose, but certainly not both of us! You've got to believe that!'

'With an empty basement to show for it? Come now, miss!'

'The girl was slim and mid-blonde,' Cynthia continued deliberately. 'She was wearing evening dress of an amethyst shade. The man attacking her was my fiancé, Terence Hewlett. He asked me to come here tonight.'

'Your *fiancé*?' the constable repeated, astonished.

'That's what I said. Where he's gone — and the girl and the laboratory, I just don't know. But something has got to be *done*! You can't dismiss this as an illusion, not when two people saw it.'

'This basement certainly belongs to Mr. Hewlett,' the caretaker put in.

The incredulity deepened on the constable's beefy face.

'And you two ladies actually saw a complete laboratory?'

'A photographic one, anyhow,' Cynthia responded. 'Not very surprising since Mr. Hewlett is a photographer by profession.'

The constable reflected and then looked around the basement once again. It only confirmed the earlier fact: that the place was quite empty, unless a solitary electric bell high up on the wall could be classed as significant. Cynthia noticed the constable looking at it and she gave a little frown.

'Come to think of it, I didn't hear that bell ring when I pressed the button outside.'

'Press it again,' the constable ordered.

Cynthia stepped out into the corridor and obeyed. The bell did not react in the slightest.'

'Mm, mighty queer,' the constable decided. 'And I still think the whole thing's a joke. The only line I can take, since you insist on getting action, is for me to report it at the station and they'll decide what to do about it. Probably contact Mr. Hewlett himself and see what he has to say. Meantime, ladies, let me have your addresses.'

Both girls gave them, and the constable nodded as he closed up his notebook.

'Right! You may hear something; you may not. Depends on whether the matter is deemed serious enough for investigation.'

With that he went on his way down the long, tiled corridor, and Cynthia and Janice looked at each other, and then at the caretaker.

'How often did Mr. Hewlett come here?' Cynthia asked him.

'Can't say as I've ever seen 'im, miss. My quarters is at the further end of the passage there, and I don't interfere with the tenants unless they need me.'

'But when he had all the laboratory fittings put in you must have seen them being brought down this passage surely?'

'Not necessarily, miss. They could have been brought in from the car park end.'

'The way we came in, you mean? Yes, I suppose they could.'

'Any'ow,' the caretaker said, brooding, 'it don't look as though any apparatuses was brought in!'

'Don't you think we'd better get back home, Cyn?' Janice put in; still plainly unnerved. 'I'm plain scared of what's been happening here! If there's anything fresh the police will contact us quickly enough. Best thing you can do in the meantime is try and contact Terry and see what he has to say. He has a 'phone at his home, hasn't he?'

'Uh-huh — and if he isn't in maybe his mother or father will know where he is.' Cynthia nodded decisively. 'Yes, I'll give him a ring. Let's be going . . . '

'And I'd better lock this basement up again, I suppose?' the caretaker asked.

'Yes,' Cynthia assented. 'I don't know what's supposed to be happening next, any more than you do.'

She turned away quickly into the passage-way and Janice followed her. In ten minutes they had reached a street telephone kiosk and Cynthia quickly dialled Terry's number.

'No, Cyn, I don't know where he is,' came the voice of Terry's mother, when Cynthia had identified herself and explained the circumstances. 'I thought he might be with you.'

'By rights he should! He made an appointment this morning on the 'phone and asked me to meet him at his new laboratory in Andmouth Street.'

'New laboratory? First time I've heard

about it — But then he doesn't tell me very much.'

Cynthia sighed. 'All right, Mrs. Hewlett, thanks. I'll sort it out somehow.'

She rang off, stepped out into the street again, and explained the situation to Janice — which only served to deepen Janice's bewilderment.

'I don't see I can offer any useful suggestion, Cyn. I just can't think straight anymore. Maybe we'd better keep to my original idea and go home. We can start moving when we know something, and this district isn't *too* attractive.'

Cynthia gave a rather wan smile, too troubled to make any direct comment. She turned her steps in the direction of the street where they had left the car, and Janice fell in beside her, only too glad to be moving away from one of the most baffling experiences which had ever befallen her . . .

★ ★ ★

The fact that it was fully ten-thirty did not prevent certain youths and girls of the

East End prowling around the dim streets and empty post-blitz areas that constituted the neighbourhood to which they were accustomed. They did it most nights, unless the weather was so inclement that they had to seek recourse to a cinema or a dance hall.

On this occasion the fine drizzle did not prevent them wandering around as usual. They had no particularly immoral aim, in spite of what certain high-ranking clergy and educational officers said about them. They merely enjoyed one another's company. So it happened, then, that a half-dozen of them — three loudly dressed youths and three giggling, curvaceous maidens, were crossing what was locally known as McCarthy's Slag when they saw IT.

'Oh gosh — look!' It was one of the girls who spoke first. She came to an abrupt halt, pointing ahead of her, and since her other arm was linked round her boy friend, he stopped, too. The couple either side of them slowed down and looked ahead in surprise — then horror.

Distinctly visible in the light of the

lamp overlooking McCarthy's Slag was the upper half of a woman's body. She was practically on her side, her mid-blonde hair flowing out along the dirt and cinders. Against the blackness of the ground, and contrasted with the amethyst colour of her evening dress her skin seemed intensely white. As white as that of a corpse.

'Hell's bells,' one of the youths said — then he began hurrying forward, pausing when he was within two feet of the sprawling girl.

'Is she . . . is she dead?' One of the girls looked down at her with round eyes.

The first youth went on his knees, peered at the half-buried girl closely, then finally took hold of her wrist rather gingerly. After a moment or two he swallowed hard and glanced up at the sober faces.

'Dead all right — '

'Of course she is!' one of the other youths broke in. 'Look there — just under her heart!'

The others looked. There was a large, dark stain, black against the amethyst colour of the gown.

'Murder!' One of the girls gave a little gasp. 'Somebody's either shot her, or knifed her, and then tried to bury her in this rubbish. Maybe got scared off or something — Don't touch anything, none of you! I remember something about never doing anything to a dead body.'

'Tell the police!' one of the youths said quickly. 'I'll go and find a bobby: rest of you stay here and stand guard . . . '

And within ten minutes the dead mid-blonde was a police problem, with the teenagers each giving their statements and not feeling too happy in the doing. To them this was a vastly new and decidedly scarifying experience: to the police it was a routine job, so routine indeed that the details were gathered in an almost matter-of-fact manner during the night, were made up in the form of a dossier, and finally found their way to the office of Mortimer Garth, C.I.D. Chief Inspector, secretly proud of the fact that he had not one 'Case Uncompleted' in his files . . .

2

It was ten o'clock the following morning when Mortimer Garth entered his dingy office at the Yard, overlooking the Thames Embankment. He tugged off his overcoat, threw his somewhat faded trilby up on the peg, then ambled across to his desk ... As usual he looked disgruntled — not because he had a permanent grudge against life, but because dyspepsia was an ever-present complaint.

'Morning, Whitty,' he growled, throwing himself into the swivel chair.

Detective Sergeant Whittaker, his right-hand man, returned the greeting from his own desk in the corner, then continued his study of a sheaf of reports that he had clipped together.

'Seems to me,' Garth said, snipping the end from a cheroot and lighting it slowly, 'that things are slipping. Been quiet for over a fortnight now. Much more of this and they'll put me on the retired list . . . '

He belched gently, thumped his chest, then scowled at the morning's correspondence. Jamming his cheroot at the corner of his thin-lipped mouth he began a perusal of uninteresting reports and orders from high up.

And Whittaker in the corner still frowned over the report he had put together.

'What the devil are you reading there?' Garth questioned at last. 'If it's from a girl friend, it shouldn't be. Remember, you're married.'

'Yes, sir. A fact I don't find easy to forget . . . '

Whittaker got to his feet — a tall, crisp-moustached man still in his early thirties. Efficient enough but lacking that one divine spark of imagination that could have earned him promotion long since.

'This report's got me puzzled, sir,' he explained, coming over. 'Interesting — yet baffling.'

'Let's have it. If it wasn't baffling it wouldn't have been shoved on to us. What is it? Robbery, murder, arson, or what?'

'From the looks of it — murder.'

'Mmm.' Garth took the clipped sheets and scanned through them intently. He was a pale blue-eyed man with bulging cheek muscles and a square chin. Very little escaped him, even though there was a disarmingly casual air about him.

'Mid-blonde in an amethyst evening gown found stabbed to death on McCarthy's Slag . . . ' He flipped the pages until he reached the police surgeon's report. 'Knife entered the heart from above, piercing the — Oh, hell, this is routine stuff. What's so *interesting* about it, Whitty?'

'You'll find the interesting part on folio Two A., sir.'

'Stop being so damned technical, man. I've too much wind round my heart this morning to be interested in *anything*. Tell me about it instead, and I'll check the details afterwards.'

'Very well, sir.' Whittaker drew up a chair and sat down on the opposite side of the big desk. Garth lounged, his pale eyes fixed on the smoky ceiling, his short, thick hand massaging his barrel of a chest.

'Seems, sir, that the story started around seven-thirty last evening. Inquiry by the East Division police revealed that two young women — Janice Worthing and Cynthia Harwood — went to a basement photographic laboratory recently rented by one Terence Hewlett. Hewlett is the fiancé of Cynthia Harwood and she went at his invitation. When they arrived they pushed open a slide on the door of the photographic laboratory and saw beyond a murder taking place. In a word, Terence Hewlett was in the midst of stabbing a mid-blonde in an amethyst dress . . .'

'Who was later found on McCarthy's Slag. Right, what next?'

'There's a good deal in between, sir.'

'Then get on with it.' Garth bit down savagely on his cheroot.

'The two women sent for the caretaker and he opened up the laboratory. Only it was empty. No sign of Hewlett, the girl who was being murdered, or anything else. They told a constable — KL567 by number — and he couldn't believe it.'

'I should think not. Then?'

'The women left; the caretaker locked the empty basement up again, and at ten-thirty or thereabouts six youngsters near McCarthy's Slag found the mid-blonde half-buried in cinders with no explanation of how she got there.'

Garth took his cheroot from his cruel mouth, stared at the ash, then flicked it on the worn rug at his feet.

'So it's another of those blasted conjuring tricks, is it?' he demanded. 'We've had 'em before — like the case of that shipper, Hammond, who travelled fifty miles in ten minutes.'

'Yes, sir. This business isn't like that, though. This girl's body was found a mile from the photographic laboratory so no problem of distance covered enters into it. The problem *is*: how did she get out of the laboratory to be found half-buried a mile away?'

Garth twirled in his swivel chair so he was facing the somber-faced Whittaker across the big desk.

'What's the girl's name? The murdered one, I mean.'

'Er — ' Whittaker picked up the reports and riffled through them. 'Sandra Melbrane.'

'Sounds like a confection. Who was she? What was her background, occupation, and all the rest of it? Anything on that?'

'The East Division police only discovered her name first thing this morning. They managed that by the cleaner's mark on her evening gown. It was listed under Sandra Melbrane, of 18, Anthony Place, South West. They didn't go any further than that, though. South West is in our area.'

'It would be,' Garth growled. 'So the East Division boys pass the buck to us, irrespective of the fact that the body was found in their territory.'

'Still the Metropolitan Division, sir, therefore within our province.'

'What you really mean, Whitty, is that they couldn't make anything of it and so threw it in our lap. All right . . . ' Garth chewed his cheroot for a moment.

'One thing emerges: Sandra Melbrane was evidently not a girl who lived in luxury.'

'I wouldn't say that, sir. Anthony Place is pretty select: I've checked up on that.'

'Maybe it is — but a girl in high flown circumstances doesn't send her evening gown to the cleaners: she buys a new one. Any photos from the boys on the spot?'

'Yes, sir — these.' Whittaker got up and went over to his own desk. From it he brought over six photographs, taken with the usual police reflex camera. They showed the murdered girl lying in the cinders, and she had been photographed in the customary three positions, together with close-ups.

'Mmm, fairly pretty, too,' Garth commented, one eye shut against cheroot smoke. 'Damned messy business, murder, Whitty. Damned messy world altogether, in fact . . . ' He rumbled satanically and then added, 'No, the girl wasn't in the upper bracket of finance. The gown is last year's. I know because my daughter had one very similar . . . Okay, make a note that we inquire of Anthony Place later on.'

'I have done so, sir.'

Garth frowned to himself for a

moment, then picked up the surgeon's report and studied it —

POST-MORTEM REPORT ON .... DECEASED

Cause of death I ascribe to penetration of the upper wall of the heart, injury having been caused from a knife blade approximately four inches long. Death would be instantaneous. The lips of the wound where the knife entered suggest that the knife was single-bladed and driven in with considerable force from above — probably wielded by the hand of an aggressor. Impact point suggests that the killer was not of particularly robust strength, otherwise the hilt indentation on the outer flesh would have been much deeper. I have examined the body internally by X-ray process, but find no other cause than the one stated which could have occasioned death.

The woman is about twenty-five and was in good health at the time of death. I examined her at 11-17 p.m. — prior to post-mortem — and she had then been dead about five hours.

Roland K. Hanworth,

Divisional Surgeon.

'Nothing frightfully mysterious or unusual about this,' Garth said, tossing the report down. 'But that business of the photographic basement is a stinger. A 'now you see it, now you don't' sort of act!'

'Yes, sir. The two women concerned were questioned by the East Division police and repeated their declaration that they had seen murder done. Their reports are there.'

Garth gently massaged the bulges on either side of his jaws.

'Tell me something, how were the East Division boys smart enough to connect up Sandra Melbrane with the photographic basement? Where's the connection?'

'Far as I can tell, the constable who examined the mystery basement turned in his report to headquarters. One of the women had said that the girl they'd seen being murdered with a knife was wearing an amethyst coloured gown — so when Sandra turned up in a similar gown the tie-up was complete. This was evidently the woman who had mysteriously vanished from a laboratory which didn't exist.'

'And our zealous constable naturally had the addresses of the two women who'd seen the murder? Or thought they had?'

'Yes, sir. And they *must* have seen the murder, sir, otherwise Sandra's murdered body wouldn't have turned up later.'

Garth transferred his cheroot to the other side of his mouth and closed his eyes. At length he took a bottle of magnesia tablets from his pocket, tipped one on to his tongue, then stubbed the cheroot in the ashtray.

'Dead five hours before eleven-seventeen,' he mused. 'If we stop being hair-triggered we can call it quarter past eleven. That takes us back to quarter past six. And what time did the women see the murder committed?'

'Around seven-thirty, sir.'

'Something,' Garth decided, 'is rotten in the State of Denmark . . .' He reached out to the intercom and snapped it on. 'Garth here. If Dr. Hanworth has arrived yet have him speak to me, please.'

'Right, sir.'

Garth was lucky. After a moment or two the sharp voice of the indefatigable Hanworth came through.

'Morning, Mort. Rather expecting you'd call — About the girl found stabbed last night, I suppose?'

'Naturally. Your report says she'd been dead five hours. I have it on more or less reliable authority that it should be four hours. The woman was alive about seven-thirty.'

'A difference of an hour might be missed,' Hanworth said. 'You know that well enough, surely? Exterior conditions would affect the corpse, too — drizzle, cold wind — '

'Yes, yes, I know, but in this instance can't you be more specific, doc? It may be one of those cases where things hang on pinpointing the hour of death.'

'Sorry, Mort. I'm a surgeon, not a magician. Four or five hours fits.'

'Some help that is,' Garth growled, and switched off. Then his pale eyes glinted towards Whittaker. 'What about the knife which did the deed? Or fingerprints?'

'No trace of either, sir. The photographic basement has also been examined and there's nothing there either.'

Garth got to his feet. 'This is too much like chasing rainbows for my liking, Whitty. Time we did a bit of questioning — Oh, this basement owner — Hewlett. He is the one who was seen stabbing Sandra. What about *his* statement?'

'Here, sir . . . ' Whittaker picked it up. 'He denies all knowledge of the affair though he admits he knew Sandra fairly well. His statement doesn't give us much clue as to what Sandra's background was. Hewlett denies he invited his fiancée, Cynthia Harwood, to visit his laboratory. In fact, he says he hasn't got one — except the one beneath his establishment in West Norton Street. He's been in business there for some time.'

'Hasn't got one!' Garth groaned. 'The things we run into . . . Right! He's number one. Come on . . . '

Within fifteen minutes their official police car had brought them to Terence Hewlett's photographic establishment. It was a fairly modern shop with wide windows, chromium edges, and a good deal of costly equipment gleaming under neon lighting ... His freshly lighted cheroot at an angle Garth entered the shop and looked about him. Immediately a young man with a rather too-stiff collar and decidedly spotty face came forward.

'Can I help you, sir?'

'I imagine so. I want a word with Mr. Hewlett, if he's here.'

'Yes, sir, he's here. A moment, please ... '

The spotty youth vanished into distant quarters and at length returned with a tall, good-looking man of about thirty. He had serious, dark eyes and a pleasant enough smile.

'I'd like a word with you, sir ... ' Garth briefly displayed his warrant card.

Terry hesitated, looking at the grim faces. At least both Garth and Whittaker were in plain clothes, but they nonetheless had that certain stamp about them

'My office is here,' Terry said, motioning. 'Please come this way.'

Garth and Whittaker followed him into the office and he closed the door behind them, motioning to chairs.

'Make yourselves comfortable. A drink, perhaps?'

'Not whilst on duty, sir.' Garth rubbed his chest slowly and continued, 'I don't suppose this visit is a surprise. The East Division police have already taken a statement from you, I believe?'

'Concerning Sandra? Yes. They came to my place last night — and a pretty nasty shock it was, in the middle of the night — especially to my mother and father. Apparently they'd got my address from Cynthia.'

'Cynthia being Cynthia Harwood, and your fiancée?'

'That's right.' Looking troubled, Terry half perched against the nearby roll-top and glanced briefly towards Whittaker as he unobtrusively took notes.

'I am not here to make a charge or anything of that nature,' Garth explained. 'I'm fact gathering. There'll be an inquest on Sandra Melbrane in a few days time, and it will be adjourned until the police inquiry is complete. This is part of that inquiry ... Now, what can you tell me about the girl?'

'Not much, I'm afraid. I knew her in a friendly way because she was one of the leading lights in our local cine club, of which I am the chairman — to say nothing of being general factotum.'

'An amateur actress, you mean?'

'Yes and a good one, too. She was also well connected with the Yellow Room Players, a local dramatic group. Her normal line of business was that of a mannequin.'

'I see,' Garth murmured. 'And did she live alone, with her parents, or what? Can you tell me?'

'She was what is popularly called a 'bachelor girl' and had a flat at Anthony Place.'

'And you and she — forgive my bluntness — did not mean anything to each other?'

Terry's eyes sharpened. 'Certainly not! Cynthia Harwood is my fiancée. I thought I'd made that clear.'

'You did,' Garth conceded, with a curiously cold amiability. 'Well now, let us pursue something else . . . I understand that you took over the tenancy of a basement in Andmouth Street and turned it into a photographic laboratory, asking Miss Harwood to come along last night and see the place?'

'I did neither,' Terry retorted. 'I never had the tenancy of any place but this, and I extended no invitation to Cynthia last night.'

'According to her statement you rang her up yesterday morning.'

'I know she said that: the East Division police told me. But I don't understand it. The only thing I can think is that somebody hoaxed Cynthia.'

'Mmm . . . ' Garth rubbed his jaw bulges and scowled at the carpet. Then, 'What exactly *did* you do last night, Mr. Hewlett?'

'I stayed here and finished a batch of prints which were behind time. The customer rang up about them around quarter to six and made an urgent demand. So I just had to comply. Matter of fact I'd told Cyn the night before about those prints wanting doing, which was one reason why I made no date with her.'

'And can you prove you stayed here and finished the prints?'

'I'm afraid not. I worked alone. I realise it means I have no alibi for last night, but it's the truth, believe me.'

Garth reflected. Whittaker's hand remained poised over his notebook, and for a time there was silence. Then Garth gave his reluctant, frozen smile.

'Frankly, Mr. Hewlett,' he said genially, 'you seem to be in something of a mess, don't you? You can't *prove* you were here last night; you knew Sandra Melbrane quite well, and Miss Harwood's word that you rang her up is as good as yours that you *didn't*. No way of checking that since dial telephones don't tell us anything. Damnable invention in some ways.'

'At least that supposed laboratory of mine can be checked,' Terry said impatiently. 'The tenancy cannot be in my name because I don't know anything about it.'

'Possibly,' Garth said, 'we can settle that right now. I have it in the records that the L.C.C. are the landlords, so let's see what we can do. May I?' He reached out to the 'phone on the desk.

'Help yourself.'

Garth did so, and after a good deal of cross-talking with the municipal authorities finally located the department he wanted.

'Chief Inspector Garth here, C.I.D.,' he explained gruffly. 'You have a list of tenancies of basements in Andmouth Street. What is the name of the tenant of number forty-seven?'

Terry lighted a cigarette nervously. Whittaker stroked his close-cropped moustache and considered his shorthand.

'Thanks,' Garth said briefly, and rang off. Then his pale eyes looked up at Terry. 'The name is Terence Hewlett . . . How do you account for that?'

Terry sighed. 'I just don't! The whole damned thing is a put-up job by somebody! I tell you I don't know anything about it! Best thing you can do is ask the authorities what the tenant looked like when he paid the rent and took over.'

'Doubtless I'll get around to that in time,' Garth conceded, rising. 'Meantime, sir, I apologise for having been a nuisance.'

Terry looked surprised. 'Then — you're not arresting me, or anything?'

'I said earlier, this is only a preliminary inquiry.' Garth paused and gave a dour glance, then picked up his smouldering cheroot from the ashtray, where he had left it whilst phoning. 'You still insist, Mr. Hewlett, that Miss Melbrane meant precisely nothing to you?'

'Of course I do! That's a fool question when Cynthia is my fiancée.'

'Is it?' Garth grinned round his cheroot. 'Not every man is so faithful to one woman. My only reason for repeating the question is to find some *motive* for the killing of Sandra Melbrane. No murder ever happened without a motive: there had to be one in her case. The usual motives are — love, impulse, money, blackmail, or plain fear. Sandra could not have excited any of those emotions in you, I suppose?'

'Certainly not!' Terry looked contemptuous.

'Mmm.' Garth gave a shrug. 'Right then — and thanks. I'd advise you not to leave the district without informing me at the Yard. 'Morning, sir.'

Back in the patrol car again Garth sat in the bucket seat and scowled through the windscreen.

'By jiminy, it's hell,' he muttered.

'Bit complicated, sir, yes,' Whittaker agreed.

'I don't mean the case, man; I'm talking about wind. It's giving me the gripe. Damned if I know whether these weeds give me wind or whether I get wind because I don't smoke enough of 'em. Vicious circle, my lad. And what did you think of him?'

Whittaker was accustomed to these roundabout approaches and had his answer ready.

'Likeable, sir, after a fashion. Seems straightforward. But that doesn't mean he's innocent. I don't forget Thurby the Rector, who looked like a saint, and he'd put away six women in a row.'

'Right now,' Garth grunted, 'I could put away six bitters in a row and blow this dyspepsia of mine to Hades . . . Well, that's Hewlett, far as we've got. Better skip around to Cynthia Harwood's place and see if we can discover what she's talking about. Motive, my lad; that's what's stumping us.'

'And the missing weapon, sir,' Whittaker reminded, and with that switched on the ignition, switching off again when fifteen minutes later they had reached Cynthia Harwood's home. It lay in the select quarter of the suburbs with a trim maid doing the honours.

'This girl evidently doesn't lack for much,' Garth murmured, as he and Whittaker were left alone in the lounge.

'No, sir, apparently not. On the verge of the idle rich, maybe.'

'Mmm. The Devil finds some mischief still for — Ah, good morning, Miss Harwood. It *is* Miss Harwood?'

Garth rose as Cynthia entered, and as was usual where a woman was concerned he subdued his physical troubles and presented a fixed smile. Only the penetrating coldness of his eyes could never be masked.

'I am Miss Harwood, yes,' Cynthia assented seriously. 'I gather you gentlemen are from the Yard?'

'Chief Inspector Garth, madam.' Garth exhibited his warrant-card. 'And Detective Sergeant Whittaker. I understand the East Division police have already interviewed you concerning the Sandra Melbrane business?'

'Oh, was that her name? They didn't know it when they came during the night . . . But please sit down.'

'Her name was established this morning,' Garth explained. 'The inquiry has now passed to me, Miss Harwood. Did you know the murdered girl at all?'

'No. Never saw her before in my life.'

'Did Mr. Hewlett ever mention her name to you?'

Cynthia reflected, then looked vaguely wondering. 'Matter of fact I can't be sure. He *may* have done, in connection with a cine club, or something.'

'Ah!' Garth looked vaguely pleased. 'Yes, she was a leading light in a cine club run by Mr. Hewlett. However, let that rest for a moment. Tell me exactly what you and Mrs. — er — '

'Mrs. Worthing, sir,' Whittaker put in.

'Yes! What you and Mrs. Worthing saw through the door slide last evening.'

In detail Cynthia described exactly what she had seen and Garth listened in attentive silence. There was no look of definite incredulity on his face: only profound interest.

'Quite remarkable,' he commented finally. 'Does any explanation suggest itself to you?'

'None, I'm afraid. It certainly could not have been a delusion because Janice saw it as well.'

'You saw — er — Read it back, Whitty.'

'Photographic laboratory — dim lighting. Large table with a girl in amethyst evening gown struggling for her life. Terence Hewlett with the knife attacking her and finally killing her. A bench with a considerable number of bottles and — '

'In fact, quite a room full,' Garth broke in, with his hard, inscrutable grin. 'Yet only emptiness when the door was opened.'

'Nothing more,' Cynthia confirmed. 'A

bell high up on the wall — which wouldn't work. And an ordinary light overhead, the switch for it being beside the door.'

'That confirms the East Division police report,' Whittaker put in.

'After which Mr. Hewlett, Sandra Melbrane, and everything else vanished into thin air. Obviously that could not happen.'

'Obviously not,' Cynthia confessed. 'For myself there was *one* solution which occurred to me — '

'Yes?' Garth's pale eyes slitted at her.

'Something photographic, perhaps. But then, that would need a slide or film projector and there wasn't a trace.'

'That solution occurred to me also, Miss Harwood, but as you say, the absence of apparatus rather takes the gilt from the gingerbread. However . . . Tell me, Mr. Hewlett rang you up yesterday morning, I understand? About what time?'

'Around nine-thirty.'

'From his home, or place of business?'

'I've no idea, but it sounded very much

to me as though he was using a call-box. I heard the sound of the 'A' button being pushed when I answered.'

'Mmm . . . ' Garth reflected. 'And this Sandra Melbrane — You don't know of any connection which she might have had with Mr. Hewlett?'

'No. As I say, I didn't know her personally at all.'

Garth smiled and rose to his feet. 'Thanking you, madam, for being so explicit. I'll probably be in touch with you again later. I would caution you not to leave the district without first consulting me.'

'Of course, Inspector. Sorry I can't be more helpful.'

With that, Garth took his departure, Whittaker at his side. The sergeant was looking dubious when they were once again in the car.

'Not getting anywhere very fast, sir, are we?'

'No. There seems to be an excellent defensive screen being put up, and somehow we've got to break it down. Tell you what you do; drive me to Andmouth

Street where I can look that basement over, then go and get up-to-date statements from Janice Worthing and Sandra Melbrane's place of work. Find out from 18, Anthony Place all you can about her, particularly if she kept a date with Hewlett last night. Also get to know if anybody at her place of work might have wanted her out of the way. Motive, Whitty — that's what we've got to find.'

'And, if we can, the weapon which killed her, sir.'

'Dammit, I know that! Why keep bringing it up?'

'Because — with due respect — you don't seem to be making much effort in that direction.'

'I'll work in my own way, my lad, if you don't mind. That weapon, wherever it is, will be in its hiding place for long enough yet. Probability is, the murderer has destroyed it, or something. Anyway, get moving. I want some coffee before I go much further.'

Garth duly had his coffee, and then carried out his pre-arranged programme. In fact, it was towards five-thirty in the dismal winter afternoon before he finally landed back at the Yard, having phoned for a squad car to convey him from the other side of the city. Whittaker had already arrived and was busy at his typewriter. Since he was working on something in foolscap triplicate it was evident he was typing the statements of the various people interviewed, ready for their signatures.

'Any luck, sir?' He looked up momentarily.

'Hell's own,' Garth grunted, dragging out a cheroot and lighting it moodily. 'Tramped my damned feet off, stared around until I've got spots before my eyes, and nothing to show for it. Y'know, Whitty, this business is damned clever. You don't appreciate it until you're up to your chin in it.'

'Yes, sir,' Whittaker agreed. 'I rather thought it wouldn't prove an open and shut case ... I got Mrs. Worthing's statement as you asked, and it merely verifies what Miss Harwood had to say. As to the murdered girl herself, she lived in rooms at 18, Anthony Place, and I had a long conversation with her landlady. Seems Sandra was a decent, clean-living girl — far as the landlady knew, anyhow. Had to be more or less, rigid in her behaviour being a mannequin. Ate little, took a good deal of exercise, and slept whenever she could.'

'Very unexciting,' Garth growled, rubbing his chest. 'What else?'

'Nothing to show that Hewlett dated her up last night, but she *did* have a message from the Elite Model Salon asking her if she'd care to have a word with the proprietor thereof. Some kind of a job as a model.'

Garth inhaled from his cheroot. 'Go on, man!'

'That's all, sir. Possibly she kept the appointment; possibly she didn't. She was out when the message came, but her landlady took it down. About six o'clock Sandra went out, gowned to perfection — Oh, yes, that was a point! The message asked that she be in evening dress, preferably something of a violet or purple shade to match a certain colour scheme.'

'Did it now!' Garth had commenced to

look interested. 'That would suggest that whoever sent the message knew Sandra had a gown like that — or else a most astonishing coincidence took place. The message was by 'phone you say, since Mrs. Landlady took it down?'

'Yes — by 'phone.'

'Man or woman's voice?'

'Woman's. She said she was the secretary for the Elite Salon, sir.'

'Right!' Garth clamped his palms down on his desk edge. 'Get the Elite Salon before they shut. This looks interesting.'

'Unfortunately,' Whittaker said sadly, 'there *isn't* an Elite Salon. It was the first thing I was going to do — 'phone them. But they don't exist.'

Garth sat back again in his swivel chair. 'Somebody is trying to make this business blasted awkward! Let's see where we are to date . . . ' Rumbling gently within himself, he pawed the various reports and notes and compared them with his own scrawled observations. At intervals he spat out comments.

'Sandra Melbrane murdered by somebody who wasn't very strong. Proof of that in lack of hilt depression in flesh. Mmm. She responded to a call from a non-existent salon, and presumably a non-existent proprietor, and instead of getting a job, got herself murdered. In between this happening she got tangled up somehow with Hewlett in a laboratory which likewise didn't exist and yet was seen clearly by two women in full possession of their senses. She was still alive when the police surgeon says she could have been dead. Hewlett says he doesn't know a thing about it, but he can't prove his actions last night.'

Whittaker listened interestedly, glancing at his own notes now and again. As Garth smouldered and belched, Whittaker added his own notations.

'Hewlett says he spent the evening catching up on wanted prints. His only alibi is, that having told Cynthia he'd be busy on them he obviously wouldn't make a date with her. He didn't know he would be *that* busy on them, of course. That only came about when the client asked for them in a hurry.'

'Yes.' There was distance in Garth's

pale eyes. 'Somewhere in the recesses of my addled brain that rings a bell — but I don't know what sort of a bell as yet. Motive? None that we can see.'

Grim silence. Garth drew at his cheroot for a while, and then continued.

'After coffee this morning I phoned back to the Yard here for a detail of men to start hunting for the weapon. Any report so far?'

'Not yet, sir.'

'I hardly thought there would be. Probably the murderer took it away with him . . . Following that call to the Yard, I had a long look at that basement. Nothing could be emptier. Four walls and a ceiling of solid tiled brick. Since the tiling has come off in parts the landlord's put a coat of white distemper over everything. The door bell doesn't work: I tried that. The only thing that *does* work is the electric light. The conduit pipe to that is plainly visible along the ceiling, then dropping down the doorside wall to the switch. Out of that conjure a laboratory and a murderer, if you can!'

'Photographic, sir, as Miss Harwood suggested.'

'I know photography links up naturally with Hewlett, but you can't get a photographic effect without a camera, or projector, or slide-carrier, or something. The only other answer is that those two women are lying. They didn't see anything, but for some damfool reason insist that they did.'

Whittaker duly considered this, his feet on the earth, as usual. Finally he shook his head.

'I think they're speaking the truth, sir. Certainly, I'm sure Janice Worthing is. She's the nervous, easily scared sort — not one to invent a lie like that and brazen it out to the police.'

Garth scowled in front of him. 'Afterwards I went to the L.C.C. offices and checked up on the tenancy of that basement. It seems the tenancy was arranged through the post. Hewlett put in his application and supplied the references required — mainly bankers. But for some reason he sent the required six months' rent in advance in notes, in a registered envelope. Not by cheque. Quite legal, of course, but it suggests somehow that he didn't wish his name to appear on a cheque. He also had the receipt sent to the *basement* and not to his shop or home. Think of that how you like.'

'Somebody took the basement in his name,' Whittaker said, after a moment.

'My belief, too. But whom? And anyway, that isn't the main problem. The main problem is what monkey business went on in that basement to make things come and go?'

'Hewlett,' Whittaker said slowly, 'denies all knowledge of the basement. Has he seen the place at all?'

'I dunno. Wouldn't do much good if he did. He'd still deny any connection with it. We've two points of view here, Whitty — either somebody has taken the basement in his name and is shifting the blame to him; or else he really *did* take it and, since the murder, has thought it better to deny all knowledge of it. There *is* one point: the original application for the place was made on his own memorandum

— his photographic shop. I saw that for myself.'

'Oh, you did?' Whittaker looked bothered. 'Signed by him, too?'

'Typed — and signed by him.'

'Then we should have it checked by the typewriter at his shop and submit the signature to our caligraphists for expert opinion. That's easy enough.'

'Yes, easy enough — and we'll do it.' Garth stubbed out his cheroot and sighed. 'But without the answer to that basement we're in a mess, Whitty. It's beyond *me*, and when I get that way I start thinking about a man who looks like a bust of Beethoven . . . '

3

For a moment or two Whittaker stared in something like horror.

'Bust of Beethoven, sir? Oh, *no!* You can't mean that maniac, Dr. Carruthers!'

'Nobody else who looks like Beethoven, is there? And bumptious little nuisance though he is, he certainly knows his job when it comes to the intricate problems. This problem may have a scientific answer, and if so, Carruthers is the specialist to tackle it. We can easily carry on with the routine side of the enquiry, but laboratories and people which appear and disappear require solving by a brain more specialised than mine. 'Fraid Hiram Carruthers is the only answer. I'd thought of going out to see him in Halingford tonight, since he'll never deign to come here. Feel like joining me?'

'Of course, sir.' Whittaker tried to sound cheerful; not an easy task when he'd promised the wife to join her in watching Episode 2 of 'Hangman's Creek' on the television.

'Okay. Get him on the 'phone.'

Whittaker picked up the 'phone. 'Halingford, seven-eight.'

Halingford lay thirty miles south of London, a small town with a promising future. It also housed, in an ancient Georgian type house, Dr. Hiram Carruthers, ex-boffin and back-room boy, one of the most skilled and eccentric scientists of the day.

'*Well?*' Whittaker nearly dropped the 'phone as that shrill falsetto voice blasted at him through the receiver.

'Scotland Yard here, sir,' he announced gravely, and handed the phone to Garth. Garth took it.

'Dr. Carruthers?' he asked gently.

'Naturally! Did you expect Napoleon Bonaparte?'

Garth cleared his throat. 'Garth here, doctor. I've a matter upon which I'd like your advice. You've helped us a lot in the past with your specialised knowledge and — '

'Never mind the soft soap, Garth!

When can you be here?'

'This evening — any time to suit you.'

'Seven-thirty then. Be an excuse to have an extra brew of tea. And don't be late. My time's valuable.'

''I'll be there,' Garth cooed, and put the phone down as he muttered something under his breath. Then he jerked his head. 'Look up a train to Halingford to get us to Carruthers' by seven-thirty. After that have sandwiches and tea sent in. I've got wind in the belly again.'

Whittaker complied with the requests with his usual matter-of-fact calmness. Then as he chewed sandwiches he handed over the reports upon which he had been engaged.

'All ready for the various folks to sign, sir. Care to look through them?'

'Hell, no! I've too much on my mind. Incidentally, any news when the inquest on Sandra is to be?'

'Tomorrow afternoon at four. Be adjourned, of course, until we've finished.'

'Mmm . . . ' Garth munched steadily, his jaw muscles bulging in and out amazingly. 'Pity we have to throw this in Carruthers' lap,' he sighed. 'Got to admit the man's brilliant, but he's so infernally insulting. Seems to think us chaps at the Yard here are a bunch of amateurs.'

'Compared to him, sir, I sometimes think we are.'

Garth scowled and said no more. It was plain he did not relish the interview with Carruthers; nor was his moroseness at all alleviated when the scientist's forbidding housekeeper admitted them to the Georgian home at seven-thirty that evening. Knowing the way from past experience they went straight down the hall to the room at the rear. Garth knocked gently with his knobbly knuckles.

'Come in, dammit!' barked a shrill voice.

'Sounds in a good humour,' Whittaker murmured, and Garth threw open the door. Then he paused on the threshold, wondering how any room could possibly get into such inconceivable disorder and yet still make sense.

The main article of furniture was a massive desk with bulbous legs. Here and there the leather top was visible but most of it was smothered in all manner of papers of various sizes and colours. Like an island, a stand with twin inkwells loomed up . . . By the window wall was a row of steel filing cabinets; in a recess was a vast bookcase crammed to bursting point . . . In the grate a big fire crackled merrily, casting considerable heat towards a big armchair — and here Dr. Hiram Carruthers was sprawled, apparently at peace with the world.

'For God's sake come *in*,' he insisted. 'There's a draught. Dammit, I know the room's untidy. So's *any* room where there's any work going on!'

Garth cleared his throat slightly, jerked his head to Whittaker, and together they advanced into the Bedlam, Whittaker closing the door behind him. Only then did Dr. Carruthers rise to his feet — an amazingly short man with all the assertiveness of a bantam. His stature, however was compensated for by the astounding strength of his face. Force radiated from every part of it. The massive head and brow, the jutting lips and jaw, the curved nose, the relentless sky-blue eyes. Nearly white hair and tufted grey eyebrows gave Carruthers the look of an ancient patriarch — or, coming nearer home, a bust of Beethoven.

'Well?' Carruthers asked, shaking hands. 'What's all the trouble about?'

'Sandra Melbrane,' Garth growled. 'You'll have read about the business, I suppose.'

'Naturally, if only to see what kind of a mess you boys of the Yard make of it — Sit down.'

Meekly Garth and Whittaker obeyed. Carruthers remained standing.

'Care for tea? And don't dare say no!'

He dived his hand into the mountain of papers around him and produced a bulging teapot with a woollen cozy. It looked very much like a shrunken vest around a portly stomach.

Neither Garth nor Whittaker said anything as pallid muck was poured into three cups. They accepted the offering with as much good grace as they could muster, marvelling silently at the relish with which Carruthers drank the tepid stuff.

'Well, go *on!*' he challenged at length putting cup and saucer aside. 'What's so puzzling about Sandra Melbrane? Got a knife through the heart, didn't she?'

'That's the least puzzling part,' Garth said. 'The bit we *cannot* fathom is how two perfectly sane young women saw a laboratory in which a murder was committed, and, without moving from the spot, saw everything disappear — murderer, murderee, lab, the whole works.'

Carruthers did not look surprised — but then he never did. The mystery that could astonish him had not yet been conceived.

'That bit wasn't in the papers,' he commented. 'And considering the way it sounds I'm not surprised. Be a bit more explicit, can't you?'

So Garth explained all over again, pausing at intervals to accept verification or note-reading from Whittaker. Carruthers listened attentively, staring fathoms deep into the bright fire.

'The first explanation which comes to mind is a photographic angle,' he said.

Garth laughed shortly. 'I thought of

that, but the basement was empty. *Empty!* You can't produce a photographic effect without some kind of instrument with which to do it.'

'So says the genius of Scotland Yard! And rightly! No doubt that. You are absolutely sure there wasn't anything?'

'Of course! We made a thorough examination. Four bare walls and a ceiling. A bell which didn't work and a slide on the door — '

'Ah, yes, that door slide!' Carruthers narrowed his eyes for a moment. 'Seems odd to me to put a slide on the *outside* of the door, so just anybody could push it aside and look at what was going on within. Usually they are on the inside. Did you inquire if the door had always had a slide, or was it put there after Hewlett took over? If it *was* Hewlett who took over.'

'Matter of fact, I didn't enquire about that. Naturally, I assumed that — '

'*Assumed!*' Carruthers interrupted in scorn. 'That's the trouble with you Yard fellows: you assume far too much. That should have been your first point of enquiry.'

'I can't think why.' Garth looked puzzled. 'What's the door slide got to do with it?'

'Off hand I don't know, but in a puzzle like this every part should be fitted into place, including the door slide. You come to me with half a story and expect some brilliant kind of answer. I can't make bricks without straw.'

'Forgetting that for the moment,' Garth said stiffly, 'how do you imagine Sandra Melbrane got from the laboratory to the rubbish dump, killed in identically the way seen by those two girls. The murder *did* happen, Carruthers: it's a matter of piecing together the bits between.'

'At a rough guess — though at this stage I haven't much idea what I'm talking about — I'd say that Sandra Melbrane was never *in* the laboratory, nor the murderer either. Those two young women saw *something* — no doubt of that — but it was far removed from the real thing. The only thing I can suggest is that I have a look at that basement and see if I can fit into place the bits you fellows have missed out. Bunglers!'

Carruthers snorted, struggling to his feet. 'That's what you are! Have some more tea?'

'Thanks, no,' Garth responded, with a glassy smile. 'Not much in our line.'

'Then it should be. Helps you concentrate ... Anyway, let's be going. My assistant, Gordon Drew, is on holiday with his wife at the moment, so I'll drive the car myself.'

Just what this meant, Garth and Whittaker found out shortly afterwards. Carruthers drove his powerful racer as though he were an entrant for Silverstone, taking full advantage of the fact that with a chief inspector and detective sergeant with him he could not be had up for breaking the speed limit. In accordance with which they reached Andmouth Street in record time and marched down the dreary, tiled tunnel that led past the various offices.

'Who the blazes would want to rent business offices down here has me beaten, anyway,' Carruthers commented, striding along with a black homburg on the back of his white mane. 'No accounting for taste, I suppose.'

He stopped when Hewlett's laboratory was reached, and the somewhat bored-looking constable doing guard duty saluted promptly.

'Nothing happened?' Garth asked him briefly.

'Less than nothing, sir.'

'Okay. Fetch the caretaker.'

This short-sighted individual was duly located and unlocked the door. Carruthers looked him up and down, then:

'You're in charge around here, I take it?'

'I am that, sir, yes.'

'Right, then. See this slide on the door here? Did Mr. Hewlett put that on for himself or has it always been there?'

The caretaker scratched his head. 'Matter of fact, sir, I don't rightly know. I've never looked at these doors particular-like. It may 'ave been there; it may not. Certainly I don't remember any bangin' or thumpin' to put a hole through the door.'

'Banging and thumping, as you choicely put it, would not be essential,' Carruthers pointed out coldly. 'An ordinary soldering iron plugged into the lamp socket up there could burn a square out of the door quite silently. Never mind. You obviously don't know the answer.'

'No, sir — 'fraid I don't.'

Muttering something about 'blasted incompetence' Carruthers strode cockily into the basement, switching on the light as he did so. Then he stood surveying, Garth and Whittaker immediately behind him and both of them noting that all was exactly as it had been on their last visit.

'Couldn't be emptier, could it?' Garth demanded, lighting a cheroot.

Carruthers did not reply. He began a slow prowl, inspecting the tiled walls carefully after he had removed the distemper covering with his thumb nail. There was certainly no doubt about the fact that they were tiles, but here and there they had fallen out and been filled up with cement to bring them level with their neighbours.

'Notice the odd shape of this wall?' Carruthers glanced briefly over his shoulder at the two Yard men. 'Curved in the shape of a bow. Unusual thing to find in a basement. They usually have perfectly straight walls.'

'Evidently conforms to some oddity in the shape of the building,' Garth said.

'Perhaps. I am never one to accept the obvious solution: that is why I am a specialist . . . You!' Carruthers looked sharply towards the wondering caretaker. 'What lies beyond the curve of this wall?'

'Swimming baths, sir. Underground baths.'

'Mmm, I see. Yes, that would possibly account for the unusual layout. And the curved wall is directly opposite the door in full view of the door slide.'

'Right,' Garth confirmed, one eye shut against cheroot smoke. 'I can't see that that means anything.'

'Trouble with you, Garth, is that there are very few things you *do* see, otherwise you wouldn't always be pestering me to solve your problems for you.'

Garth smouldered silently and Whittaker drowned a grin behind an unexpected coughing attack — by which time Carruthers had wandered to the door and stood looking at it. When he closed it from the inside, however, and tried to look through the slide he was far too short.

'Get a stool or chair, or something,' he told the caretaker, and the old man shambled off obediently.

'Nothing to be gained from that slide,' Garth said, shrugging. 'I've already looked through it.'

'Which, I regret to say, is no criterion. I suppose it did not dawn upon you that there may be great significance to be drawn from the fact that that curved and completely unblemished wall faces this door slide?'

'Significance?' Garth gave a dour look. 'Doesn't seem the least significant to me.'

Carruthers gave his infuriating, know-all smile and then turned as the caretaker returned with a stool. Immediately the little scientist mounted it and peered at the slide. Since it was closed on the outer side of the door it was evidently not his purpose to see through it. Instead he examined it very carefully, occasionally resorting to a pocket lens.

'For your information, Garth,' he said

finally, 'this door slide was set into a slot which was *burned* out exactly as I theorised. That way no noise would be made and since the caretaker's quarters are some distance away he'd probably not smell the burning wood.'

'No, I didn't smell nothing,' the caretaker assented, though it seemed pretty clear he hadn't the least idea what he was talking about — or Carruthers either.

'Does that get us any nearer a laboratory which isn't?' Garth asked, irritated.

'Possibly. If you will pursue the inference further you will realise that whoever rented this basement — Hewlett or otherwise — wanted the slide put in specially, and didn't want to attract attention whilst fixing it up, either. So far, so good . . . '

Carruthers descended from the stool, opened the door, then closed it behind him as he went into the corridor, dragging the stool after him. Garth chewed his cheroot and aimed a dubious eye at Whittaker. Being a man of fair wisdom Whittaker maintained silence, then both he and Garth jumped as Carruthers shot the slide back on the outside of the door. Turning, they beheld his piercing blue eyes looking in at them dispassionately. It was funny, somehow, but neither of them dared show it.

'Mmm,' the little scientist said, as he mooched back into the basement. 'The slide is clear glass.'

'Even we could see that,' Garth growled. 'And anyway what else did you expect it to be?'

'Pink and green, as a matter of fact.'

'Eh?' Garth tried not to look stupid, but he did just the same. And it was typical of Carruthers that he did not explain himself any further just then. Instead he recovered the stool once more and, by standing on it, he was just able to reach the bell on the top of the right hand wall. He studied the disappearance of the wires behind the wall and then frowned.

'Where do these wires go?' he asked the caretaker.

'Far as I know, sir, they're laid between the tiles — sunk into the niches as you might say, and then mortared over.'

Carruthers nodded, apparently finding no fault with the explanation. Descending from the stool he went outside to the bell push and pressed it. As on previous occasions, the bell did not respond.

'Very nonsensical,' he commented. 'Trouble is taken to set a perfect slide in the door, yet the bell — most important thing of the lot — is ignored. Let's see now . . . '

Garth and Whittaker rather wished they could. They stood in the basement doorway and watched as Carruthers fished a fountain-pen torch from his pocket and flashed the beam on to the bell push. At first sight there was nothing the matter with it — but this by no means satisfied Carruthers. With a small pocket screwdriver he went to work and removed the screws holding the bell, revealing beneath that both wires were broken.

'That's funny,' Garth said, frowning. 'Makes you wonder how those wires could have got like that. The two wire ends still screwed into the bell push sockets, yet broken off at precisely the same place.'

'Broken off is right,' Carruthers agreed grimly, busy with his lens. 'Take a look through this.'

Garth looked. At the end of a minute he had satisfied himself that the smooth tile in which the bell push was normally screwed was minutely scored and scratched as though a blade had exercised a sawing movement.

'Well?' Carruthers asked. 'Satisfied?'

'Looks to me as though a thin blade has been inserted between the tile and the bell push, thereby cutting the wires and rendering it inoperative. But what the blazes for? Why render a bell useless in such a clumsy way? Been easier to unscrew the damned push and pull the wires away.'

'That would depend on how much time the 'cutter' had. I think,' Carruthers finished, 'we can take it for granted that somebody was very determined this bell push should not be used. What we need to do now is connect up the wires and see what happens.'

He did so, and pressed the button. Immediately the bell rang stridently.

'That,' he said, scowling, 'is not what I had expected!'

'Why not?' Garth demanded. 'Dammit, you expect a bell push to ring a *bell*, don't you?'

'Normally, yes — but here we have an abnormal situation. I rather expected something else would happen.'

'For instance?'

Carruthers sighed. 'Consider the facts, man, and do a bit of thinking for yourself! The need to stop the bell ringing could not be so desperate as to demand the cutting of the wires from outside — hastily, with the blade between tiles and bell push. The need must have been much stronger — perhaps to break a connection which would bring into action certain photographic apparatus, set in motion by the normal pressing of the bell button.'

Garth gave a start. 'You mean that perhaps . . . ' He frowned hard and bit his cheroot. 'Hell, but that's hard to accept! You mean that pressing the bell button started the illusion — or whatever it was?'

'I believe so. And the cutting of the

wires prevented the illusion from being repeated at a most inconvenient time. Hence my puzzlement. I expected this re-linking of wires to start up the apparatus: instead it performs its normal function. It surely isn't possible that I — Carruthers — can be *wrong* in my theory?'

'None of us is perfect,' Garth murmured dryly.

Carruthers did not seem to hear him. His homburg on the back of his head he was gazing down the tunnel. Everybody waited for something to move on the face of the deep.

'I agree that a photographic possibility is the only logical one to explain this business,' Garth said, after a moment, 'only I can't find any possible *clue*. For instance, those two young women must have seen the whole thing looking incredibly life-like. If it were on a screen — even if in colour, as it was — they'd know it wasn't the real thing.'

Carruthers gave a brief glance. 'Not if they saw it through polaroid glasses. It would be three-dimensional and have the necessary depth! Use your noodle, man!'

'I am doing!' Garth returned, stung. 'Polaroid glasses! Dammit, you don't suppose they came equipped with *those*, do you?'

No. I expect the slide did it for them, but I haven't figured exactly *how*.'

'The slide? But — ' Garth looked at it. 'It's clear glass! No polaroid business about it.'

'Not now — and that deepens the puzzle. If, though, one half of that slide were green and the other half pink, or red, and there was projected on to that flawless slightly curved wall a double three-d film image, they would think they were looking at an actual scene. The whole thing's quite possible; it is the brilliant way in which it is covered up that is sharpening my already razor-keen wits.'

Garth took out his cheroot, stamped on it, then turned the slide and examined it. He peered steadily into the basement through the clear glass and then gave a grunt.

'Mmm, I see what you mean. If bisected by two colours — red and green

— it *would* make a perfect polaroid slide. Just no *other* way of seeing into the basement.'

'Exactly. Now consider that idiotic plate on the door — 'Please look through inspection shutter and if the red light is on there will be a delay in answering door.' Have you ever come across an order like that before, especially in conjunction with photography? Why, light accidentally streaming through this slide into the darkroom could ruin everything! Quite probably the girls never thought of that: they obeyed the order and then saw the vision sinister.'

Garth massaged his bulges. 'All this would be explainable if only we could get our hands on some apparatus! Something to show what did the trick!'

'Yes . . . ' Carruthers stepped back into the basement and surveyed the wall in which the doorway was set. Then he added, 'Whatever there was in the way of projection, if we accept that as our basis, must have come from this wall and been projected upon the curved wall facing us. That suggests there must be some kind of opening *somewhere* in this wall.'

If there was, it was amazingly well hidden, for it failed to reveal itself to all the minute probings of the three experts. The distemper was unbroken; no portion was lighter than the other. In fact the whole wall was absolutely intact.

'Clever,' Carruthers admitted. 'Decidedly clever.'

He looked speculatively at the ceiling, but here again there was the same unbroken smoothness. There was no necessity to climb up to it to make a special examination: it was quite clear nothing peculiar existed up there. And the floor . . . that, too, was solid concrete and incapable of being faked in any way.

'We're doing wonderfully!' Garth commented sourly. 'Four walls do not a prison make — but they do here as far as our imagination is concerned.'

'Mmm,' Carruthers agreed absently, looking at the big 15-amp power plug low down on the wall on which the doorway was set. Then whatever thought passed through his mind remained unexpressed. Instead he sighed.

'In any case,' Garth said, after a moment, 'it would not be possible to put a projector between the inner and outer wall there. The machine would be too big, and the spools would take up far too much room. Can't be more than four inches width between the walls.'

'True,' Carruthers agreed, with unusual mildness for him, then after a moment he turned aside to the constable and caretaker who were still hovering.

'This basement has been left absolutely untouched and unvisited since the police took over?' he asked the constable.

'Absolutely, sir. Nobody's been near.'

Carruthers looked at the caretaker. 'What's under this basement, if anything? Or is it the limit?'

'There's the boiler rooms, sir, for the central 'eating.'

'There are, eh? We'll have a look at 'em.'

The purpose of visiting the boiler rooms was quite beyond Garth and Whittaker, but they accompanied Carruthers and the caretaker just the same. Down in the depths the heat was considerable, since the heating system was in full operation. Not that Carruthers was in the least interested in the furnaces: he moved around and studied the ceiling. At intervals there were six-inch-long gratings.

'For ventilation?' he asked, and the caretaker nodded.

'There's narrow tunnels between this ceiling and the floors of the basements above. Hot air goes through there, sucked by a fan on the vent at the side of the building. At the opposite end of the building there's another fan what blows in fresh air.'

'Get me a ladder,' the little scientist ordered brusquely, and until it came he spent the time carefully pacing the floor and measuring something for himself.

'I suppose it would be talking out of turn to ask what you're up to, Carruthers?' Garth asked.

'No; but it wouldn't do you any good, because I don't intend to answer until I'm sure. That way I can't be caught out.'

With his gnome-like grin Carruthers turned to the ladders as they were set up for him, and in a matter of moments he had climbed to the third grating from the left. Under the pressure of his hands it immediately lifted inwards into the narrow ventilating tunnel. He set it on one side in the shaft, pulled out his fountain pen torch, and flashed the beam into the draughty, hot darkness.

'Anything doing?' Garth asked quickly.

'Yes. Two ends of newly bared wires that don't lead anywhere — at least, not at the moment. Tell you more in a moment.'

For Carruthers to get his head into the opening and thereby see the shaft properly was impossible, so he fished within his enormous overcoat until he had produced a small hand mirror. By its aid he was enabled to see wherever he needed through the simple process of reflection.

'Very interesting,' he said finally, which didn't convey very much. 'I'll be back in a moment . . .'

He descended the ladder and returned to the basement above where the constable was still on duty. And it was the constable who watched in some amazement as Carruthers deliberately went to work to rip away the supports of the wires leading to the bell. As the caretaker had said, the wires were laid in the cement between the tiles, stapled into position and covered over again with thin plastering and white distemper. Under Carruthers' reckless treatment, however, the wires were finally torn free of their moorings until they came to the corner of the room. Here, instead of continuing on the doorside wall, they vanished through a minute hole.

'We're having a great deal of fun, constable,' Carruthers grinned, as he reflected.

'Yes, sir. So it would seem. Anything I can do?'

'Not that I know of . . . '

With that, Carruthers returned to the boiler room. Garth and Whittaker, mopping their faces, looked at him enquiringly, but he still did not satisfy them. Once more he mounted the step ladder and peered long and earnestly into the shaft, using his mirror and fountain pen torch as before — then, apparently satisfied, he returned to the floor.

'Is all this too profound for us to understand, or what?' Garth asked irritably. 'It gets irksome just watching and getting no clue.'

'All right, make what you can of this: Normally, the wires from the bell push drop down behind the tiled wall into this ventilation shaft. They then turn left along the shaft and, about six feet away — which is the distance from the door to the bell-wall in the basement above — they go upward again and then disappear through a hole. That hole is practically at the top of the basement wall — the wall that has the bell. Thereafter the wires go to the bell. Nothing unique about that. What I can see of this shaft *all* the bell wires are laid in that way.'

'Well?'

'The bell wire has been cut in two and hastily rejoined — which is why the bell rang when we fastened it up properly on the bell push above. But there is also a length of wire with bared ends that doesn't start from anywhere or *go* anywhere. Now I've looked more closely I see that it's top end is hooked over a small, jutting piece of beam, which obviously is part of the floor support above — no, more correctly it must be part of the *tunnel* floor support. That is immaterial. What signifies is this length of strong wire which has been left behind.'

'With bared ends?' Garth looked baffled 'But what is its purpose?'

'Well, my guess is that the bared ends don't mean a thing. It just happens to be a length of strong wire and as such would make an excellent support — Wait! Probably in cutting the wire through the ends became bare, the other half of the wire being taken away. This piece apparently stuck too well and could not be released quickly enough.'

Garth thumped his chest and coughed gently. Then he said frankly, '*You* know what you mean, but I'll be damned if we do. Eh, Whitty?'

'Bit confusing, sir, certainly,' Whittaker admitted, and Carruthers glared.

'It's as simple as *this*!' he said deliberately, smacking his palm with the flat of his other hand. 'One — somebody decided to use the bell push as the means of making a contact to an apparatus, probably a projector. That meant that when the bell push was pressed the apparatus came into action. Two: the apparatus itself was hung in this shaft space, held by the length of wire already mentioned. In removing it apparently only half the wire could be obtained in the limited time, so the remaining half had to be left behind. The bell wires were hastily relinked, but even then they didn't work until they were properly joined at the bell-push end. *Now* is it clear?'

'Uh-huh,' Garth acknowledged grudgingly, then he looked sharply at the caretaker. 'Can *anybody* get down here if they wish to?'

'Nothing to stop 'em,' the caretaker shrugged. 'Certainly no reason to lock this place up. Nothing can be stolen.'

'And it's quite a distance from Hewlett's basement,' Garth mused. 'Yes, the responsible one *could* take a chance at that.'

'You mean *did*,' Carruthers snapped.

'And got away with it, too. This boiler room is just round the angle of the passage and out of sight of the guardian constable. The apparatus which was used was smuggled in and smuggled out without anybody being the wiser.'

'The step ladders would be needed,' Whittaker pointed out. 'Where would those be located?'

The caretaker jerked his head towards the adjoining basement, the door of which was obviously wide open. In fact the whole stage was set for anybody to do as they pleased.

'These gratings always been movable?' Garth asked.

'Aye,' the caretaker acknowledged. 'They 'ave to be to allow for reg'lar inspection.'

'Fits in very nicely,' Garth admitted, 'but it *still* does not solve the most puzzling point of all. How did those two women see a laboratory which didn't exist?'

'I have the answer to that one, too,' Carruthers responded, smiling mysteriously, 'but before I go to work on it and give you a practical demonstration — my invariable practice — I must be dead sure I'm right. Hiram Carruthers never produced a failure, remember.'

Garth signed. 'Okay — so we have to wait until you've worked everything out. What do we do in the meantime?'

'Find out more about Sandra Melbrane and her relationship with Hewlett. I think he's lying when he says she didn't mean a thing to him. As far as the knife that killed Sandra is concerned, I don't think you'll ever find it. The killer will have completely done away with it. Not that it signifies. When you can prove how the murder was committed and who committed it, the presence of the weapon is not essential — or have I misread the Judge's Rules?'

'No, you've got it straight,' Garth conceded. 'Very well then, we'll dig up something more concerning Sandra if we can, and when you're ready you'll fit the last pieces into this puzzle-basement?'

'Naturally. We have here a most ingenious killer, even one with a scientific turn of mind, but *not* one with the ability to defeat *me* . . . '

4

Not feeling at all sure just how far he had progressed in the basement problem — and certainly not able to follow Carruthers' complicated line of reasoning — Garth returned to more normal fields next morning, commencing with a second visit to Terence Hewlett's photographic shop. Terry was present, sorting out various cameras, and his lips compressed a little as he saw Garth and Whittaker coming towards him. Immediately he handed over to his spotty-faced assistant and indicated his private office.

'Well, gentlemen, what this time?' He looked at Garth and Whittaker as they seated themselves.

'I have reason to believe,' Garth said, removing his cheroot from his teeth, 'that you were not entirely explanatory enough on the last occasion concerning your associations with Miss Melbrane. Perhaps you'd care to elaborate some of your earlier statements?'

Garth was using nothing else but bluff, but Hewlett was far too inexperienced to notice the fact.

'I have nothing to add, inspector. Sandra was merely a friend and a useful actress for the cine club.'

'And you maintain the association stopped right there?'

'Definitely! Why should you think otherwise?'

'I think otherwise because of the complete absence of motive in this business. Apparently Sandra was a quiet-living girl — indeed she could not afford to be much else with her health and reputation to maintain as a mannequin and model. She had no real enemies, or at least none vicious enough to think of killing her. The only other person who seems to be at all dominant is your-self . . . ' Garth leaned forward, his pale eyes cold and hard. 'Be absolutely frank with me, Mr. Hewlett. The consequences may be quite serious for you otherwise.'

Whether this would work or not Garth had not the least idea, but at least it was worth trying. To his satisfaction there was a reaction of sorts. Hewlett stood hesitating beside the desk, obviously having a struggle to make up his mind.

'To a certain extent,' he said at length, 'Sandra and I were fond of each other. But not in the infatuated sense. It was platonic — like brother and sister.'

Garth nodded rather dubiously. 'Whatever you may have called it, it would have looked to the outside world as though you were 'that way' about each other. Correct?'

'I suppose so, yes.'

'Especially to the other members of this cine club of yours?'

'I'm not concerned with what they thought.'

'But I am, Mr. Hewlett. In my business I have to see things as everybody else would see them. Let us say, at random, that some other young man had a fancy for Sandra and secretly objected to your attentions to her. He could, if his mind worked that way, have decided to put an end to Sandra rather than you should have her.'

Whittaker looked vaguely astonished. This was quite the most corny postulation Garth had made in some time.

'I imagine,' Hewlett said, smiling bitterly, 'that the hypothetical young man would have been more anxious to put an end to *me*, and get Sandra for himself. Only there *isn't* such a young man.'

'There isn't? Thanks for telling me.'

Hewlett looked troubled. Apparently it had only just dawned on him that he had been as good as tricked into admitting that there were no jealous young men in his cine club.

'Concerning this club of yours,' Garth continued, 'How many members have you?'

'Oh, ten or twelve maybe. Nearly all of them, amongst the men, are middle-aged. I'm about the youngest, and the next youngest is my assistant back in the shop there. Quite a few women, though, including my fiancée of course.'

'Your fiancée? You mean she's a regular member?'

'She's there when needed, anyway. Very interested in all we do in the photographic line.'

'How often did she and Sandra Melbrane meet?'

Terence Hewlett reflected. 'Half a dozen times, perhaps.'

Whittaker exchanged a covert glance with his superior and Garth returned his cheroot to his teeth.

'I think you'll be interested to know, Mr. Hewlett, that your fiancée told me she'd never met Sandra, though she had a vague recollection you'd mentioned her now and again.'

'A vague recollection! But that's utterly absurd! Cynthia and Sandra knew each other quite well: they were the backbone of the club.'

Garth mused over something, then, 'Ever done anything in three-d, Mr. Hewlett? For your cine club, I mean?'

'I've experimented with it many a time. Ordinarily I wouldn't be able to afford it, since the cost of the stereo-lenses for the camera is pretty stiff, but being in the business I can borrow freely.'

'Quite so. What kind of scenes do you shoot?'

'There were several of Sandra showing

off various gowns, which were later projected at a private mannequin parade. I thought it might do me some good photographically. Then there was a short quarrel scene, between Sandra and myself, which Cynthia herself photographed. So she can hardly say she doesn't know Sandra! The other scenes were exterior and — '

'You didn't ever photograph one in three-d, which represented a laboratory, with yourself apparently murdering Sandra with a knife?'

'No! Never!' Hewlett gave a hard glance. 'Think what you like, inspector, but that's gospel truth. I know just what you are thinking . . . '

'Do you?' Garth asked dryly.

'You are thinking that the mystery of my so-called laboratory in Andmouth Street, which I have really never seen, might be explained by three-dimensional photography and projection. You are thinking that the original scene was first photographed and then projected . . . You're wrong — as far as the scene being photographed is concerned, anyhow.'

'For some reason,' Garth said slowly, 'I am inclined to believe you, Mr. Hewlett.'

'Thanks very much!'

'And that being so, I feel it incumbent on me to branch off on a fresh tack — Oh, did anybody ever borrow your camera with its three-d attachment at any time?'

Hewlett shook his head. 'I never permitted that — not even to Cynthia. The equipment is far too valuable and I couldn't afford the loss if anything happened.'

'I see. Well, thank you, Mr. Hewlett.' Garth got to his feet. 'Oh, a thought! Was Mrs. Janice Worthing a member of your cine club?'

'No. She's Cynthia's best friend, of course, but I think her only interest is her home.'

'I see.' Garth jerked his head to Whittaker and turned towards the door as Terry Hewlett moved to open it. There was a serious expression on the young man's face.

'Look, inspector, I know I'm pretty

deeply involved in this, but can you tell me *how* deeply? Whatever you might think from the things I've said — and particularly the fact that I held back about my friendship with Sandra — I did not kill her!'

'Just why *did* you hold back so much in telling me about her? Wasn't very sensible of you, you know.'

'No, I suppose it wasn't. Matter of fact I was scared. You suddenly appeared and turned on the heat and I thought if I said too much about Sandra you'd start to arrest me, or something . . . I feel I know you better now.'

'Good!' Garth gave his wintry smile round the cheroot. 'As for how deeply you are involved . . . Well, I'm not in a position to say much. I'd still caution you not to leave town without my permission. Incidentally, strictly off the record, what kind of health have you?'

'Health? Why, pretty good. Haven't needed a doctor since I was a kid.'

'Mmm.' Garth appraised Hewlett silently. 'Yes, I can credit that, too — Well, see you again, maybe. Let's move, Whitty.'

Whittaker nodded, and there was a puzzled look in his eyes as he accompanied his superior to the car. It was still there as he settled at the wheel.

'Rather a roundabout conversation, sir, wasn't it?' he asked curiously.

'Frankly, Whitty, I hadn't much idea what the hell I was talking about — at least not to begin with. I warmed up a little as time went on.'

'Yes, sir. But what has Hewlett's health got to do with it? Or were you merely being conversational?'

Garth scowled and threw the stub of his cheroot through the car's open window.

'Since when was I ever conversational? I talk for a reason, or not at all. I simply wanted to discover if Hewlett is weak or normally strong. All things considered, he appears to be reasonably strong. I'm remembering that the knife blow that killed Sandra was delivered by somebody of 'not particularly robust strength.' That doesn't seem to fit Hewlett unless he deliberately pulled his punches — and as a killer that wouldn't be a very bright thing to do. Incidentally, what do you make of Cynthia Harwood saying she didn't know Sandra?'

'Pretty puzzling, frankly, but she must have had her reasons.'

Garth said nothing for a moment. He stroked his bulging jaws and gazed moodily through the window upon the busy traffic. Then finally he made up his mind.

'Get going to Janice Worthing's. I want a few more words with her.'

'Janice Worthing's?' Whittaker looked surprised. 'You don't mean Cynthia Harwood's, do you?'

'No,' Garth retorted sourly. 'Get going!'

Whittaker obeyed and, to Garth's satisfaction, Janice Worthing was at home when they arrived. The seriousness of her definitely pretty face more than suggested that she was expecting trouble — a fear that Garth did his best to alleviate by smiling genially.

'Sorry to bother you, Mrs. Worthing, but so far I haven't made your acquaintance . . .'

'No — no, that's true.' Janice led the

way into the small but homely lounge. 'It was the sergeant here who interviewed me.'

'Correct. And this won't take very long . . . I believe you know Mr. Hewlett, Miss Harwood's fiancé?'

'Yes, indeed. And do sit down, please . . . I know him quite well. Very pleasant chap he is, too.'

'Is he now?' Garth was still looking genial, his variable approach to the opposite sex. 'Would you say he is a man who enjoys robust health?'

'Well — er — ' Janice looked momentarily embarrassed. 'I would not say I know him *that* well, inspector. Certainly, what I have seen of him, he never seems to ail anything.'

'Good . . . Now, regarding this extraordinary business where you and Miss Harwood saw Mr. Hewlett attacking Sandra Melbrane with a knife. Can you describe to me exactly what you did see? As detailed a picture as you can remember.'

'I've already done that. The sergeant took it down.'

'To be sure, but that was strictly for the records. I would like to know a good deal more. You are quite certain that the girl you saw being murdered in the basement was the same one later discovered on McCarthy's Slag?'

'To all intents and purposes, yes.'

'Why "to all intents and purposes"?' Garth asked. 'Can you not be *certain?*'

'Not without seeing the woman who was discovered on the Slag. I read about it, was given a full description by the police, but I haven't actually seen the body. Nor,' Janice finished, with an obvious horror, 'do I particularly want to.'

'Your reluctance is quite understandable, madam, but for the sake of evidence I'm afraid you'll have to take a trip to the mortuary with us. After the inquest later today the body will be buried, and it will then be too late.'

'Yes, I suppose,' Janice admitted, troubled. 'But is it not enough that both women — or the *same* woman wore an amethyst coloured evening gown? That couldn't be coincidence, surely?'

'Most unlikely, I confess, but it *could*

be. Identification of the body will settle that. Sandra's landlady has already identified the body as Sandra's, of course, but that is beside the point. I have got to know that the girl in the mystery basement and Sandra were one and the same.'

'I see. I suppose Cynthia couldn't identify the body instead? The very thought horrifies me.'

'She will also be required to identify it later today. *Both* of you must do so . . . Now, if you'd please describe again just what you saw in that basement.'

Janice sighed and began to explain in as minute detail as she could. Garth listened for a while, then interrupted her.

'You saw Mr. Hewlett quite clearly, then?'

'Fairly clearly.'

'That's rather vague, Mrs. Worthing. I gather there was only the single light on, the one overhead, and that it was casting a *pinkish* illumination. Would you call that an ideal glow in which to be definitely certain of features?'

'By no means,' Janice shrugged. 'I can

only say that the man appeared to be Terry Hewlett. In fact it must have been! Cynthia herself said so.'

'Never mind what *she* said,' Garth said patiently. 'What was *your* impression? Imagine for a moment that you saw that scene without Miss Harwood being there. Would you have said positively that you were looking at Terence Hewlett?'

'Not positively, no,' Janice admitted. 'I suppose it *could* have been somebody else. There are thousands of men of Terry's build and appearance. Nothing unique about him.'

'Mmm . . . Singular, too,' Garth continued, distance in his eyes, 'that when you entered the mysteriously emptied basement the light was ordinary white instead of pink.'

Janice looked vague. 'I suppose he must have changed the bulb or something before disappearing with — with the murdered girl and the rest of the stuff.'

Janice's voice noticeably hesitated, either because she was conscious of the fantastic nature of her statement, or else because Garth's eyes were fixed inexorably upon her.

'That,' Garth said, 'is the obvious conclusion. We are decided then that you could not say for sure that the man was Terence Hewlett?'

Janice nodded slowly, at which Garth appeared to be satisfied once more.

'That being so, Mrs. Worthing, I shall not need to trouble you any further — Oh, one thing! Did *you* ring the bell upon arrival at the basement, or was it Miss Harwood?'

'She did all that. After all, the whole business was her responsibility: I merely went along as an escort. She didn't like the neighbourhood.'

'Either you went as an escort, or a witness,' Garth said ambiguously. 'Time alone will show that.'

With that he took his departure and sat pondering when the car had been gained.

'She appears genuine enough, sir,' Whittaker commented presently. 'And it also seems pretty obvious that there's now a distinct doubt that Terence Hewlett *did* commit the murder.'

'I have had the greatest difficulty in believing that he did,' Garth muttered. 'There's something about him which rings true in spite of the fact he resents being questioned. His resentment is only natural reaction, perhaps. Nobody likes having his private life probed.'

'Then this person who looked like him? You think that *he* — whoever he is — may have done it?'

'At the moment I'm not even going to attempt to answer that one. What I am going to do is make a thorough examination of Sandra Melbrane's rooms — or room, as the case may be. You only inquired into her private life? You didn't make any search of her belongings?'

'No, sir, I didn't — but I did warn the landlady that the room must be left undisturbed until she had police permission to do otherwise.'

'Fair enough. All right, let's see what we can find.'

'Just what have you in mind?' Whittaker questioned, switching on the ignition.

'Matter of fact I'm a bit cloudy on that, but it is possible that a girl like Sandra

Melbrane, accustomed to keeping all manner of dates as a mannequin and model, might have kept some kind of diary as advance warning to herself. If the man in the laboratory act was not Hewlett, but somebody else, we've got to shift heaven and earth to find him. Sandra might have noted down some kind of photographic date.'

'You're dead settled on the notion, then, that the basement act *was* photographic?'

'Certainly I am — and so is Carruthers, if only he'd hurry up and show *how* it was done.'

Whittaker nodded as he drove steadily through the city traffic. When eventually they arrived at 18, Anthony Place, where Sandra had had her room, Garth wasted no time in identifying himself to the portly landlady.

'Glad you've come, inspector,' she said. 'I don't want to keep that room closed and untouched any longer than I can help. I'm having to stand out of useful rent.'

'Maybe so, madam, but that is unavoidable. Which is the room?'

'Number six on the first floor.' The landlady unfastened a Yale key from the small bunch of them hanging at her waist. 'Here you are, sir.'

'Thanks. Come on, Whitty.'

Once he had the door of the dead girl's room open, Garth stood on the threshold, looking beyond. The room was a combined one, and thoroughly neat and tidy. One half was roughly divided into a sleeping section, and the other half into a living portion. The sombre winter light picked out well-polished, solid furniture and a considerable number of trinkets and artificial flowers that bespoke the femininity of the one-time tenant.

'Writing desk over there, sir,' Whittaker said at length.

Garth nodded and strode across to it, leaving Whittaker to make a thorough search in other directions. The writing desk Garth found to be unlocked — nor was there any key — so presumably Sandra had not been at any pains to keep things secret.

Assiduously, Garth went to work, sorting through correspondence, bills, and numberless odds and ends that told nothing. In the course of his activity he came across a bank pass book, practically up to date, which credited the late Sandra with the sum of £207. Evidently she had not been a girl of any great financial resources . . . Then at length Garth found what he had been hoping for — a diary bound in black leatherette. He opened it quickly and studied the dates.

Those entries that were purely personal he promptly skipped, but his attention remained centred on items which obviously referred to the cine club. They went back several weeks and appeared on the Wednesday of each week. The entries said: *Appear as Cathy — Blue Silk . . . Cathy again; left parting. Cathy tonight. Remind Terry about toplight.* And so on.

Garth searched further through the gold-edged leaves, then he presently gave a little murmur of satisfaction. He was looking at an item for exactly a week previous to Sandra's death. Whittaker came across and looked too —

Wear amethyst evening gown and all

trimmings tonight for special murder scene for outside cine club. Three-dimensionally, it ought to be good. Check on time by ringing Riverside 2910.

'Looks interesting,' Whittaker commented.

'More than looks it, my lad. It is! Special murder scene in three-d in amethyst evening gown! For an outside cine club. What's an *outside* cine club, anyhow? Out-of-doors?'

Whittaker smiled faintly. 'No, sir. It means a club out of the immediate district. Maybe they wanted something special. Riverside 2910 might solve a good deal.'

'Once we're out of here we'll ring 'em. No need for the landlady to know everything. You find anything useful?'

'Afraid not. Not that it matters considering what you've found.'

Garth nodded and led the way out of the room. The landlady was hovering as a good-sized presence in the hall as they descended the stairs.

'Can I let the room yet, inspector?' she asked anxiously.

'I'm afraid not, madam. Sorry to be awkward about it, but that room must not be touched until everything concerning Miss Melbrane is satisfactorily cleared up. Oh, here's the key. And another thing,' Garth added, as he reached the bottom of the stairs, 'I'd like to know a little more about an appointment made by the Elite Model Salon with Miss Melbrane. You took the message I believe?'

'I did, yes. It was from the salon's secretary. A woman.'

'Yes, I have that information in the sergeant's record of your statement. Can you give me any idea what kind of a voice it was? Refined, ordinary, uneducated —?'

'Definitely educated! It couldn't be anything else from a salon, could it?'

'From a salon, no. The point is, madam, that that call was a hoax. There is no such establishment as the Elite Model Salon, and whoever made that call was the one responsible — or mainly responsible — for luring the unfortunate Sandra to her death.'

The landlady looked shocked. 'That's a

horrible thought, inspector. I wish I could tell you more.'

Garth sighed. 'So do I. The unfortunate thing is that that message would most certainly be made over the automatic exchange and there's no way of tracing its origin.'

Looking disgusted he continued on his way to the front door, then something suddenly seemed to occur to the big landlady.

'Would it help you if you heard the message repeated?'

'Not much, madam. I know it already.'

'I mean the actual speaker on the line . . . '

For once in his life Garth started, and Whittaker rubbed his crisp moustache quickly.

'The actual speaker?' Garth repeated, astonished. 'How can that be?'

'I forgot to mention it before,' the landlady apologised. 'I have a lot of tenants here, as you realise, and since my husband is out a lot there are lots of times when I'm out, too — '

'Naturally.' Garth looked irritated.

'How does that apply?'

'Well, when I'm out there's many a telephone call might get missed, so I had the radio shop install a tape recorder. On the T-E-L plug and remote control it starts itself up when the bell rings and tells the caller to speak the message and not expect a reply as it's a tape recorder.'

'That's right enough, sir,' Whittaker confirmed, quickly. 'Quite ingenious. The circuit made when the receiver's lifted is cut out in this case and operated from the phone mechanism itself. The electrical impulse of the bell ringing starts up the re-order and transmits its tape message. Then it automatically changes to 'Tele-Micro' and records whatever message comes over the line.'

'Everything but cook, eh?' Garth grinned. 'Come to think of it, I've heard of such gadgets on a recorder but never come up against one . . . I assume then,' he asked, looking at the landlady, 'that the message came on the tape whilst you were out?'

'It did, yes. It was the only message, as it happened. When a message is given the tape rewinds to the original part, which says 'Speak your message and expect no answer,' and — '

'Yes, yes — but where is this message? You haven't destroyed it?'

'Erased it, you mean?' The good woman looked knowledgeable. 'Not I! I let a whole reel get used up before I clean it off. Just a moment, gentlemen.'

'This,' Garth said, as the landlady waddled away down the big hall, 'may really amount to something! One of those strokes of luck which rarely come the way of a long-suffering cop.'

'Yes, sir. May be very useful.'

Before long the landlady was back, carrying in her arms the recorder. Whittaker took it from her and set it down on the hall table.

'Now, inspector, it links up to the phone like this — '

'Yes, madam, I am sure it does — but my interest is in the recorded message. If you don't mind?'

'No, of course I don't mind. Here it is . . .'

After some fiddling with the tape

spools and an adjustment of the speed control the landlady had the instrument as she wanted it. Then with definite triumph in her eyes she stood listening — and so did Garth and Whittaker.

'I am speaking on behalf of the Elite Model Salon of Empress Crescent, South West. I am the secretary of the establishment, and the proprietor, Mr. Manning, wishes to know if Miss Melbrane would be interested in becoming a model for a brief period. This would be a photographic commission. If Miss Melbrane *is* interested, would she kindly meet Mr. Manning at the corner of Maddox and Chepstow Streets at six-fifteen. Mr. Manning will be there in his car, and the journey to the Salon's photographer, which is not far from Maddox Street can then be made. Also, will Miss Melbrane kindly wear an evening gown of amethyst or purplish colour in order to match the photographer's layout.'

There was a click and the message ended. Garth stood frowning, massaging his chest gently.

'I can only assume Miss Melbrane

needed money,' he said at length. 'I wouldn't have allowed any daughter of mine to answer a call like that without full initial inquiry.'

'I thought the same,' the landlady sighed, switching off the recorder. 'None of my business, though, Sandra knew how to look after herself — or at least she thought she did until she was murdered.'

'I'll take that tape, madam, if you don't mind. It will probably be useful at headquarters.'

The landlady hesitated, then seeing she had no alternative she rewound the tape and handed the spool across.

'Thanks.' Garth took it and handed it across to Whittaker. 'We may see you again yet, madam. In the meantime thanks for your co-operation. You'll get this tape back later.'

The woman nodded, and with that Whittaker and Garth descended the front steps to their car at the kerb.

'Yard, sir?' Whittaker asked, switching on.

'Yes. We've got to see if we can knock any sense into what we've discovered.

There's also Riverside 2910 to deal with.'

Whittaker nodded and started the car forward. Garth sat hunched in the front bucket-seat, rumbling at intervals and thumping his chest.

'To quote one, Alice,' he said at length, 'this grows 'curiouser and curiouser'. The voice which gave that message doesn't sound to belong to anybody we've met yet.'

'No, sir — but I'd submit that voices aren't difficult to disguise, especially over a telephone. It's useful, I suppose, to have the actual voice which spoke the message but unless we find who owns it we're no better off.'

'We've just *got* to find who owns it!' Garth snapped. 'That person can tell us everything we want to know! And if I remember rightly, Maddox Street and Chepstow Street are very close to McCarthy's Slag. It's more than likely that the unfortunate Sandra kept the appointment, was stabbed to death, and then left on the Slag.'

'Minus her coat, or whatever she was wearing,' Whittaker pointed out. 'Obviously she wouldn't go out on a winter night in an evening gown without *some* covering. Wonder where her coat or wrap went?'

'I dunno. Same way as the missing knife, I suppose.'

'Maybe I'm wrong,' Whittaker said, after a while, 'but I do get the feeling that we're neglecting one very likely culprit in all this . . . Cynthia Harwood. I'm surprised you haven't mentioned her more, sir.'

'That I haven't mentioned her doesn't say I haven't thought about her, my lad. I haven't forgotten the fact that she said she didn't know Sandra Melbrane. Maybe she should be more closely cross-questioned on that. Anyway, there's no need to run out and see her: we can find out all we want when she and Janice Worthing have a look at Sandra's body for identification purposes later today. We'll fix it when we get back to the Yard.'

Whittaker nodded and drove on steadily; then after a while Garth's voice came again.

'Stop at the Anchor Café. Time we both had some lunch. I need some food to kill this blasted gripe.'

5

When Garth returned to headquarters after lunch he was in one of his rare genial moods. His dyspepsia had forsaken him for the time being and he was, however transiently, at peace with the world and ready to tackle the problems still before him. Unfortunately for him his bliss was shattered when, on entering the office, he discovered Dr. Carruthers lounging in the worn hide armchair, his homburg on the back of his white mane and a foul-smelling pipe jutting from his teeth.

'About time,' he grunted. 'I never saw anything like you boys! If you're not sleeping you're eating, and if you're not doing either of those things you're sitting thinking. Why the hell don't you get some *action*?'

'I have been doing,' Garth returned bitterly. 'Of sorts, anyway.'

'Of sorts? Huh! Such as?'

'I've got Sandra's diary, a tape

recording of the person who asked her to meet the proprietor of the Elite Salon, and I've as good as proved that Mrs. Worthing didn't actually see Terence Hewlett in the basement, but somebody else. I don't call that so bad for one morning's work.'

'I'll grant you're right, *if* you can make it all fit into place. As far as I'm concerned I've done something really useful — *and* I worked all night to do it.'

Garth and Whittaker were silent. Carruthers was always fond of advertising the fact when he had spent all night on a problem. What he did not take into account was the fact that he had almost superhuman energy.

'Solving the problem of the basement, I suppose?' Garth asked, settling in his swivel chair.

'Naturally. You don't suppose I meant the Tombs of Egypt, do you?'

'No.' Garth gave a morose glance. 'Well, what caused the basement illusion? It was photography, of course?'

'Certainly it was, with the final answer lying in the — '

Garth muttered something as the telephone rang. He snatched it up impatiently.

'Yes? Garth speaking . . . '

'Dickinson — East Division police here, inspector. We've found the knife that killed Sandra Melbrane, or at any rate it's reasonable to assume it *is* the one. Also a satin lined evening wrap and one of the latest type hats.'

'Good!' Garth's eyes gleamed. 'Where were they?'

'Buried in another part of McCarthy's Slag. I thought I might as well keep my boys at it since they were working to a fixed plan. Now I'm glad I did, for the search has proved fruitful. Shall I send the stuff over for Dabs to inspect?'

'Yes — soon as you can. What kind of a knife is it?'

'Most ordinary one you could imagine. The sort of kid's hunting knife you'd pick up in any general store of the Woolworth variety. There's rust on the blade and what are possibly dried bloodstains. That's for your pathology department to determine.'

'Fair enough,' Garth conceded. 'Send the stuff over as fast as you can . . . Nothing else, I suppose?'

'No. I've been having my boys search around for footprints, but whoever dragged that unfortunate girl's body that far, or carried it, had evidently weighed things up beforehand. The cinders on the Slag don't leave any trace of prints, nor does the pavement that skirts it. What I *was* thinking of doing was having an inquiry made in the district to try and get some news of anybody who may have been behaving suspiciously.'

'By all means,' Garth responded, 'though I don't expect a great deal of result in that direction.'

With that he rang off and looked at Carruthers expectantly.

'Sorry for the interruption, doctor. You were saying about the basement illusion. The final answer lies in what?'

'The fifteen-amp power plug.'

Garth stared. 'I — I beg your pardon?'

'Oh, dammit, man, why don't you listen?' Carruthers demanded irritably. 'The power plug is the solution to the riddle. I've experimented — not in the basement but in my laboratory — and have proved it.'

'I see . . . I think,' Garth's brows knitted. 'You mean that the power plug supplied the current which fed the projector, which — '

' . . . milked the cow with the crumpled horn, all in the house that Jack built.' Carruthers gave a malignant stare across the desk. 'No, I don't mean that at all. If you hadn't such a limited imagination you'd know exactly what I mean. In fact you'd have solved the problem for yourself by now.'

'We can't all be geniuses,' Garth said heavily.

'How well you exemplify that fact!'

Garth took a cheroot from his case and bit savagely at the end of it.

'Best thing you can do is come to the basement and have a practical demonstration,' Carruthers said. 'Let's be on our way.'

Garth shook his head. 'Much as I'd love it, it can't be done. There's an inquest at three-thirty and I've got to be there along with Whitty to say my piece. Even though the whole thing will be adjourned, it doesn't make any difference. I've still to be there. After that I'm accompanying Miss Harwood and Mrs. Worthing to the mortuary to see Sandra's body.'

'For heaven's sake, why?'

'So they can state positively that the woman they saw in the basement is the same one found on McCarthy's Slag.'

'Be more sensible if they went to the mortuary first, wouldn't it, then they can speak with assurance at the inquest?'

'It doesn't signify. You should know that the inquest in a murder case is only a formality, not a trial. The *real* evidence will be needed when, and if, we nab the killer.'

Carruthers sighed and got to his feet. 'Oh, well, since you intend to play games for the rest of the day there's no point in my staying here and offering a basement demonstration. When *will* you come? I can't be kept waiting, remember: I'm far too important.'

'By seven-thirty tonight we should be

free of immediate commitments,' Garth responded. 'That will give Whitty and I time to dash home for some tea and a freshen up, then we'll join you at the basement.'

'Food again,' Carruthers growled. 'No wonder your brains are stodgy and cluttered up. All right — seven-thirty it is, and see you're there. Meantime think again about that fifteen ampere plug. It's more significant than you ever imagined.'

Carruthers flattened his homburg more securely on the back of his enormous head, grinned cynically, and then departed.

'Fifteen-amp plug,' Garth mused, dragging at his cheroot. 'Damned if I can see the significance of that — unless you can, Whitty?'

Whittaker shook his head. 'I don't get it at all, sir. Only thing I remember is that the plug socket was embedded low down in the tiled wall, nearly at floor level, but as to what significance it has — I'm beaten.'

'The man's barmy,' Garth growled, reaching to the telephone. 'Let's try something more mundane — Hello! Get me Riverside two nine one oh.'

There was an interval of buzzing, during which Garth sat and dragged at his cheroot. Then a pleasant woman's voice came through.

'Riverside two nine one oh. Who's speaking, please?'

'Chief Inspector Garth, C.I.D., here. I am anxious to contact somebody who was acquainted with the late Sandra Melbrane. You'll have read about the case in the papers.'

'Er — yes, of course.' There was obvious hesitation. 'I think it must be my husband you wish to speak to. Just a moment whilst I fetch him . . . This is a shop, you see — the house part, anyway. He's attending to customers.'

'What kind of a shop have you?' Garth inquired.

'Groceries. Half a moment, please.'

'Groceries?' Garth frowned at the attentive but uncomprehending Whittaker; then a man's gruff voice came on the line.

'Mr. Kindross speaking. Arthur Kindross. Did my wife get it right? That you're Scotland Yard?'

'She did, Mr. Kindross. Am I to come round and see you, or can you tell me what I wish to know over the 'phone? What was your connection with Sandra Melbrane?'

'That girl who's the victim of the recent murder case? The one in the purple evening dress?'

'The same. I gather you know about her: why didn't you report everything concerning her to the police? Why wait for the police to track you down?'

'Candidly, Inspector, I wasn't aware that I was transgressing in any way. Please accept my apologies. I only saw her once, and that was only for a brief bit of filming. I hardly thought it was worth reporting.'

'*Everything* concerning a murdered person is worth reporting. This 'brief bit of filming' you refer to. What was it all about?'

'An experiment in three-dimensional photography. I'm an ardent cine fan and a big friend of Terence Hewlett. He runs an entire cine club, but I'm a lone worker using willing friends for my film scripts. They play the parts. One evening I went to Terry's film club and saw Sandra Melbrane there doing quite a good bit of acting. I decided she was what I wanted for a short murder sequence in a film of my own — '

'In three-d and colour, I take it?'

'Yes. I have a camera with a stereoscopic attachment. I asked Sandra if she'd like to help and she was only too willing.'

'I see. I assume there was a man in this murder sequence?'

'Definitely. Myself, as a matter of fact.'

'What exactly was the scene?'

'It was supposed to represent a laboratory,' Kindross replied. 'A photographic one. If you like to wait a moment I can read you the whole script.'

'No, that won't be necessary, thank you. Tell me, what was Sandra wearing?'

'An evening gown, lilac-coloured. Come to think of it, it may have been the same one she was wearing when her body was discovered.'

'More than likely,' Garth conceded grimly. 'Did you ask her to wear it, or was it her own idea?'

'I merely suggested evening dress, and she arrived in that particular one.'

'I see.' Garth dragged at his cheroot. 'Tell me, did you use reddish lighting for this murder sequence?'

'I did, yes. I thought it would suit the mood — Red for murder, and for danger. If you understand me.'

'Mm, quite. And when you had completed this murder sequence, what happened to it? I take it that it was shown on a stereoscopic projector?'

'Definitely it was. After that it was spliced into the main film.'

'Can you give me any idea who saw the completed film? I assume Sandra saw it, but who else was there?'

'Only my wife. She isn't much interested in filming, but she's a useful critic. Besides, she likes three-d films, in spite of the annoying necessity of polaroid glasses.'

'Polaroid glasses are essential, then, to the viewing of your type of stereoscopic film?'

'Definitely so, yes.'

'And only your wife and Sandra were present at the showing? There was nobody else? Not even Mr. Hewlett?'

'Well, he didn't need to come. Since he processed the film for me he'd already seen it.'

'Ah, I understand.' There was a grim look on Garth's face. 'Thank you for your information, Mr. Kindross. I'll communicate with you again if the need arises.'

Kindross rang off and as briefly as possible Garth related the details to Whittaker.

'Looks as if the bits and pieces are beginning to fit into place, sir. Evidently the scene in the laboratory was the one also seen in the basement, projected in three-d colour.'

'Exactly, and Terence Hewlett processed the double film, and would most certainly run it afterwards to check it, so he knew what it was all about.'

'It even begins to look,' Whittaker said slowly, 'as though Hewlett may know a good deal more than he's told us. In his statement he said he didn't dabble in three-d in case of busting up one of the instruments, or something.'

'*That* may be quite true. The point is that he knew all about *this* particular film, and the sooner we pinpoint him about it, the better. For the moment we can't do anything because we've that infernal inquest to attend.'

'And a few words to have with Miss Harwood, sir, if you'll forgive the reminder.'

'Uh-huh, I hadn't forgotten. I suppose those two women will have been advised about the inquest . . . Better be on our way, Whitty.'

Obviously irritated at having to shelve things, Garth at length presented himself along with Whittaker at the coroner's court. Cynthia Harwood and Janice Worthing were also there, to say nothing of the teenagers who had found Sandra's body on McCarthy's Slag . . . Not that Garth was particularly interested. To him all this was a complete waste of time, especially so since it ended as he had foreseen — adjournment pending further police inquiry. Nonetheless, the routine business did give him a chance to catch up with Janice Worthing and Cynthia Harwood before they could leave the building together.

'Good afternoon, ladies.' Garth raised his hat briefly and directed a sharp glance at each woman. 'I would be glad if you'd both accompany me to the mortuary to identify the body of Sandra Melbrane with that of the girl you saw in the basement laboratory. You, Mrs Worthing, will not find the request surprising, since I mentioned it earlier. I would also have given you due warning, Miss Harwood, if time had permitted.'

Cynthia shrugged. 'I've no objection to seeing the body.'

'Well *I* have!' Janice objected. 'I think it's a horrible idea!'

'Murder is always horrible, madam,' Garth told her gravely. 'There's a police car at the kerb there, if you wouldn't mind.'

Janice kept up her muttered protests all the way to the mortuary, but Cynthia seemed to take everything as a matter of course. She still did not flinch when, at the mortuary, she was permitted to study the dead face of Sandra.

'Yes, no doubt about it,' she admitted. 'The same girl! What do you say, Janice?'

'Yes,' Janice muttered, her face averted. 'Same girl.'

'Thank you, ladies.' Garth nodded to the officer and the sheet was replaced over Sandra's face. 'Now, sergeant, if you will accompany Mrs. Worthing to the car, I have a few words to say to Miss Harwood.'

'To me?' Cynthia paused, her eyes surprised.

'I shall not detain you above a moment or two, madam.' Garth escorted her into an adjoining ante-room and closed the door. Then, 'Would you mind telling me, Miss Harwood, why you said you'd never met Sandra Melbrane, and only knew of her vaguely through Mr. Hewlett?'

Cynthia seemed to reflect for a moment and then gave a rueful smile. Although she seemed composed enough Garth could not fail to notice how she picked at her gloves, which she had not yet drawn on her hands.

'You gentlemen from the Yard don't

miss much, do you?' she asked at length.

'Be a bad thing for the law if we did, Miss Harwood. And please be good enough to answer my question.'

Cynthia shrugged. 'Funk, inspector — nothing else but. It occurred to me that if I said I *did* know Sandra and fairly well, you might even start tying *me* up with her murder, which of course would be utterly preposterous. So I soft-pedalled as much as possible. I should have known better. It was very silly of me.'

'Very,' Garth admitted, and stood pondering. Whilst he did so, Cynthia removed a cigarette from a lacquered case and put it between her lips.

'Allow me . . . ' Garth handed her his lighter in its chamois leather bag and then turned away, rubbing the bulges on his jaws. When at length he turned back again Cynthia had lighted her cigarette and was holding the lighter out towards him once more back in its chamois leather bag.

'Thanks,' Garth grunted. 'I wish I could impress upon you, Miss Harwood, the necessity for being absolutely frank when a police inquiry is made. For your own sake please see no such evasions are tried again ... And now to something else. You say it would be utterly preposterous for me to tie you up with the murder of Sandra Melbrane. I can only admit that it is preposterous if you can prove it is preposterous.'

'Well, at least I can give a good account of my movements on the fatal night, if that's any use. The sergeant didn't ask me anything about that when he questioned me — the East Division sergeant, I mean — not Sergeant Whittaker.'

'And what were your movements, madam?'

'At six-thirty I arrived at Janice Worthing's, as you know already. Prior to that I paid a visit to my hair stylist, and I was in her salon for four hours. In other words from two until six.'

'It must have been quite an elaborate hair-do,' Garth commented dryly.

'It was — a special waving process. I was sat under one of those awful things like a space helmet for nearly four hours, and Madame Ensard can very soon verify it. After that I had just time to snatch some tea — in Madame Ensard's cafétéria adjoining the hairdressers — and since she was at the same table she'll verify that fact, too. Then along I went to see Janice.'

'In your car, of course?'

'Certainly.' Cynthia looked surprised but Garth did not explain himself.

'From two until six, eh?' He gave his hard smile. 'Well, that would seem to put you completely in the clear, Miss Harwood . . . Now we'd better get along and I'll see that you and Mrs. Worthing are taken home.'

Cynthia nodded collectedly and rose from her chair. Garth opened the ante-room door for her, his eyes thoughtful. In the car Janice was waiting in the rear seat, and Whittaker at the steering wheel.

'We'll take these two ladies home first, Whitty,' Garth said, clambering in. 'On your way . . .'

'Right, sir.'

In a matter of twenty minutes this matter had been attended to, and

Whittaker started to drive back into town. As he did so, Garth brought him up to date on information.

'Seems it's time we stopped thinking things about Cynthia, then,' Whittaker sighed. 'That's a watertight alibi. You'll check on it, of course.'

'Naturally — later on. Meantime, does it occur to you it's half past five and quite dark?'

Whittaker glanced sideways briefly. 'Don't expect anything else at this time of year, sir.'

'Regarding Hewlett,' Garth branched off. 'I think we'll go and tackle him before having tea and then carrying on to the basement to meet Carruthers. We daren't be late for *him*!'

Hewlett was attending to customers when Garth and Whittaker arrived, but he rid himself of them as quickly and discreetly as possible and then came forward.

'Once again, gentlemen? What this time?'

'Maybe we'd better talk in there.' Garth nodded towards the private office. At which Terry Hewlett nodded and led the way towards it. Once within, with the door closed, he stood waiting expectantly.

'I would have liked it better, Mr. Hewlett,' Garth said coldly, 'if you had advised me that you processed a film of a murder in a laboratory for a Mr. Kindross.'

Hewlett sighed. 'So you got around to that, did you?'

'We did. What's your explanation?'

'Same as before. I didn't want to say too much in case you jumped to the wrong conclusion.'

'One of these days, Mr. Hewlett, it will perhaps dawn upon you that concealing facts from the police is not a habit to be encouraged. I understand you processed this colour film and doubtless projected it afterwards?'

'Yes.'

'How did it come about that you processed it? I thought such films had to go to the manufacturers, especially colour?'

'Usually. This happened to be some outdated stock, which wanted special

139

treatment. Once I'd done the processing I sent the film on to Kindross and I haven't seen it since.'

'But you *did* project it, for examination purposes?'

Hewlett nodded and Garth eyed him steadily. 'Were you alone when you made the projection?'

'Definitely I was.'

Garth frowned to himself. Once again he was finding himself up against the difficult problem of liking Terence Hewlett on the one hand, yet being suspicious of his statements on the other.

'Whom else did you expect to be with me?' Terry asked.

'That isn't for me to say: it's for you to tell me.'

Terry shrugged. 'Well, there it is. There just wasn't anybody else.'

Through a long interval Garth sat considering, then with a sigh he got to his feet.

'All right, Mr. Hewlett, thanks very much. Either you can't — or won't — tell me anything more.'

Terry Hewlett's response was an

indignant glance, Garth studied him again and then jerked his head to Whittaker.

'Better be moving, Whitty.'

'Right, sir.'

As usual, when they had got to the car, they held a brief conference.

'A liar, sir?' Whittaker suggested, and Garth shrugged.

'You're as wise as I am, my lad. Quite frankly, I'd expected to hear that Cynthia Harwood was also present, but evidently she wasn't. Either this business is magnificently covered up or else we're constantly barking up the wrong tree. The one thing that *does* seem to become constantly apparent in this business is that nobody gives anything away until stung into it. Understandable, but a damned nuisance to us . . . Ah, that looks a suitable café there. Better drop in for a bite — then, Carruthers or no Carruthers, I'm dashing home to tell the wife what I'm up to. In a bit she'll begin to think I'm living a double life or something . . .'

⋆　⋆　⋆

Precisely at seven-thirty Whittaker drew up the police car in Andmouth Street, and a few minutes afterwards he and Garth were entering the long underground passage which gave on to the basement offices and workshops. Outside Hewlett's basement Dr. Carruthers was seated on a portable stool drinking the muck he called 'tea' from a thermos flask.

'Three minutes late,' he pronounced, glancing at his watch. 'When I say seven-thirty I don't mean seven-thirty-three.'

Garth again had that curious feeling that he was a schoolboy in front of the headmaster.

'We were delayed: sorry. Well, everything all set for the demonstration?'

For answer, Carruthers deliberately returned the cup to the top of the thermos, screwed it down, then got to his feet. From his inside pocket he produced a pair of polaroid glasses — one lens pink and the other green.

'Look one at a time through the

opened slide in the door,' he instructed. 'Before you do so, press the bell push.'

Garth did not ask any questions: he didn't feel it was safe to do so. Putting the glasses on his nose he moved to the door, peered into the darkness through the glass slide, then pressed the bell button. Immediately he found himself gazing on the surprising sight of Dr. Carruthers himself pottering about his laboratory. He glanced up once with a sardonic grin and then measured out a beaker full of amber liquid. Around him the lighting was dim, but sufficient to pick out the colour detail.

'Hell, but it's lifelike!' Garth whispered, handing the glasses to Whittaker. 'Take a look.'

Whittaker did so, glasses on nose, and his ejaculations were sufficient to confirm his reactions. Finally Carruthers stepped forward and pressed the bell-push. Instantly all was dark.

'Fascinating, eh?' he grinned. 'Think of it! Carruthers in two places at once! You just don't know how lucky you are!'

'How's it done?' Garth questioned.

'That's the vital point,'

'It's done in exactly the way I told you — the fifteen-amp plug. You'll have gathered by now what I meant by that.'

'Matter of fact — no,' Garth sighed. 'Too busy.'

'Too dense, you mean . . . ' Carruthers moved to the door of the basement and turned the key in the lock. 'I told the officer on duty he could take a couple of hours off,' he explained. 'The poor devil looked as though he needed it . . . '

Under the little scientist's hand the light came up — and there was the basement, totally empty, its walls white and dustless. Garth looked about him quickly, but mainly towards the fifteen-amp plug. He had expected some kind of projector to be visible, but in this he was disappointed. Everything was as bare as it had always been.

'So the mighty brain still doesn't grasp the point?' Carruthers asked, with his irritating grin.

'No, the mighty brain doesn't!' Garth retorted, and he lighted a cheroot fiercely. 'Only thing I can see for it is that some kind of invisible projector is used. Possibly, even, the killer has solved the problem of becoming invisible!'

'Keep your feet on the earth, man,' Carruthers growled. 'That doesn't make sense, not even in this advanced scientific age. All right, I suppose I'll have to adopt the usual sledge-hammer tactics if it's to make any sense to you.'

With that, he reached to the light switch and plunged the basement into darkness. This done he fiddled outside the door until he had pressed the bell push. Once he did this, Garth and Whittaker found themselves amidst a confusing mirage of lights and shadows. On the slightly curved wall double images danced and played in a variety of bewildering colours, the most predominant image being that of Carruthers himself who appeared to be performing the same actions over and over again.

'Now look at the fifteen-amp switch,' Carruthers ordered, and Garth and Whittaker did so. It seemed decidedly uncanny to them, but the twin beams producing the weird pictures were angling sharply upwards from almost floor level.

'Right, I get it!' Garth cried in sudden excitement. 'You can switch off!'

Carruthers did so, and the light returned. The little scientist gave a sour glance.

'About time the penny dropped!' he commented.

'I don't remember that it dropped so damned fast with you in the beginning!' Garth snapped. 'Anyway, I get it now. The twin beams shine through the two equally spaced holes in the fifteen-amp plug. The upper hole, intended for earthing, does not even come into it.'

'Correct,' Carruthers admitted. 'A micro-projector, one of the very latest designed for the projection of short-length stereoscopic sixteen millimetre film, has twin lenses of exactly the width of the two holes in a fifteen-amp plug. As you say, we can ignore the topmost earthing hole since it does not mean anything.'

'This,' Garth muttered, 'is one of the most damnably clever ideas I've yet come across.'

'Yes, it has its merits,' Carruthers conceded, 'but it was not so ingenious that I couldn't unravel it. Anyway, come below and see for yourself how it's done.'

The whole business had suddenly assumed such an interest that Garth even forgot his indigestion. With his cheroot clamped between his teeth he pursued the diminutive scientist down the tunnel, Whittaker in the rear, and so finally to the boiler room. Since the step ladders were already in position Carruthers did not need to waste time in this direction.

'Take a look,' he said, motioning briefly. 'I've spent more than enough time with my valuable head jammed in that draughty hole.'

Garth mounted the ladders and once he had eased his head inside the opening left by the raised steel grid he beheld a small projector firmly anchored by lengths of spare wire, the wire being hooked over the end of the beam he had noticed on the earlier occasion. The arrangement was such that the twin matched lenses of the small projector were flush with two small holes in the upper wall.

By means of a little manoeuvring Garth finally had the projector to one side, and by straining to the limit he could just see through the wall holes, and into the empty basement above, almost from floor level. Satisfied, he relaxed again and looked at the projector. Upon it was an endless length of film passing over two special brackets.

'I can only repeat what I said before,' he said, coming down to the floor and allowing Whittaker to have a look. 'The whole thing's damnably clever!'

'The projector is mine,' Carruthers said, 'but whoever put the murder scene in action must have had one quite similar. Mine is a 'Trubrite' stereo-projector, so doubtless the murderer's was also. I have used a loop film for the demonstration — one with the ends joined — but the killer probably used a straight length on small spools to guard against the chance of repetition of the scene, which would have ruined everything. The bell wire was cut and rejoined to the stop-start on the projector motor, making it that when the bell was push-buttoned the motor started up, whilst a second push stopped it. After that, it was simply a matter of moving the projector away at a convenient moment and refixing the bell wire. All that was done, but one odd piece of wire, used in holding the projector in place, had to be left behind because it couldn't be pulled free in the limited time the killer allowed.'

'That,' Garth admitted, drawing hard on his cheroot, 'would appear to be it.'

'It doesn't *appear*: it *is*!'

Whittaker descended from the step ladders, his square, unimaginative face plainly surprised.

'Tremendous amount of ingenuity,' he commented. 'I'd never have thought of that in a month of Sundays. Concerning that fifteen-amp plug, doctor — did the killer fix it there, or was it there at first, do you think?'

'To the best of my belief it was there to begin with. Whilst you two have been messing about doing nothing in particular, I called on the basement next door to Hewlett's and examined it. There is a plug there, too, in the self-same position. In fact you can see the electric cables leading to the plugs all along the vent shaft. In Hewlett's case the plug was removed and wires insulated off, but the cover was screwed back, having empty space behind it.'

'And if anybody had plugged in for power the trick would have been rumbled,' Whittaker pointed out.

'And where was the chance of anybody doing that, with only the killer connected with the basement?' Carruthers asked.

Whittaker stroked his moustache and reflected. Maybe he did not think he looked obtuse at that moment but he certainly did.

'Naturally,' Carruthers continued, 'with the grating in place there was nothing to show what was going on. The caretaker could come down here and wouldn't be wise to a thing. The killer had evidently weighed everything up to the last detail before taking action — and he more or less had a free hand since this boiler room is more or less isolated from the view of the offices.'

'Yes, the whole mechanical set-up is clearly explained, Doc, thanks to you — '

'Not entirely,' Carruthers interrupted. 'You have seen how the trick was done, how the images were projected diagonally on to a slightly convex wall which heightened the three dimensional illusion. You have also seen that the angle of projection was not so sharp that it distorted the upper edge of the projected images. And lastly you have seen that the colour rendering was so sombre that no beams from the projector were observed. *But*, those two sweet young things who first saw the illusion did not come provided with polaroid glasses, and without such a device they could not have viewed the illusion so completely. Part of the puzzle, on the mechanical side, is still missing.'

'I'd forgotten that bit,' Garth admitted. 'It was done by the door slide, wasn't it?'

'That's my guess, yes — but it is clear glass. And since the slide has not been touched since the fatal evening, a constable being on guard all the time, the problem is to decide how that slide was ever of the polaroid variety. The only solution I can see is to have the door taken off.'

'What good would that do?' Garth bit into his cheroot and frowned.

'It would enable us to tip the door about and see if anything rattles inside it! There must have *been* a polaroid system, and the parts belonging to that system must have gone *somewhere*. The only conceivable place is inside the door itself, which, as long as it stays on its hinges, cannot rattle or give anything away. Since I am an ordinary civilian — technically speaking — I cannot remove the door without permission. That's up to you, Garth.'

'Okay,' Garth assented. 'Pull it down and I'll take the consequences.'

Carruthers returned to the stepladders, removed his projector, and put the grating back in place; then with Garth and Whittaker following behind him, he led the way back to the tunnel above. Before long the myopic caretaker had been summoned.

'Get this door off its hinges,' Garth ordered. 'I'll take the responsibility if the landlords say anything.'

The caretaker nodded, went to his quarters for a big screwdriver, and then set to work.

'Something occurs to me,' Whittaker said, musing, as he brushed his clipped moustache. 'If Hewlett is *not* the genuine tenant of this place we might be able to prove the fact by finding out who printed that plate on the door here. The one who gave the order seems to me to automatically be the one we're looking for.'

Garth sighed. 'Frankly, Whitty, I'm getting browned off with following false trails, or at any rate those which turn a somersault at the end. You can be sure that anybody smart enough to take this place over without ever being seen — as happened in the case of this tenancy — would easily find a way to get the plate printed without giving anything away.'

Carruthers turned from watching the caretaker taking the screws from the hinges.

'You don't mean to tell me,' he said, in

some astonishment, 'that you don't know who planned all this?'

'Knowing and proving are two different things,' Garth said moodily, dropping the stub of his cheroot and stamping on it. 'And a word of warning, sir — we're not alone.'

The little scientist glanced towards the caretaker, and in his next statement he lowered his voice.

'I've not followed the ordinary police routine in trying to discover the culprit, of course — that's essentially your job — but it's as clear as day that whoever pressed the bell push, once to start the projector and once to stop it, is the one we're looking for.'

Garth smiled moodily and rubbed his chest. 'That occurred to me, too. Cynthia Harwood, of course.'

'Obviously!'

'I wish it were. Trouble is, it doesn't fit. She's got the best watertight alibi ever . . . '

6

For a moment or two there was silence, broken only by the caretaker as he swore blackly at the resistance of the screws. Garth made a cautioning signal.

'No place to discuss anything,' he murmured. 'We'll go into the details later.'

Evidently Carruthers was not in the mood to raise objections for he said no more. When at last the caretaker had the door removed he held it and glanced at the scientist questioningly.

'What do I do with it, sir?'

'Drag it into the basement and turn it on its side.'

The caretaker muttered something but nonetheless did as he was bidden. Once this was done, Carruthers stepped forward and with surprising strength for one so small lifted the entire door and jolted it back and forth violently. As he did so there was a curious sliding, banging sound, like a chunk of wood in a cigar box.

'That sounds hopeful!' Garth exclaimed, brightening from the gloom into which dyspepsia had again plunged him. 'How to get at the inside of the door: that's a point!'

'Not to me,' Carruthers returned. 'Let me see now . . . '

He examined the edges of the door minutely and then gave his infuriatingly superior grin.

'As I thought! Rotten workmanship. The door's hollow — just a framework with panels fastened to it. The nails are covered by the varnish.'

'So that's why you lifted it around so easily!' Garth exclaimed. 'After the struggles of our caretaker friend here I thought — '

'All our caretaker friend needs is a course of vitamins,' Carruthers said, glancing towards him. 'Anyway, that's beside the point. Your screwdriver, my friend, if you please.'

The caretaker handed it over, then he watched with some misgivings as Carruthers ruthlessly prised away the panelling from the frame. It screeched horribly as the nails lifted, but Carruthers did not go the whole way. Once he had enough room to allow of his arm getting inside the door he fished within the panelling carefully and at length brought into view a length of glass, which though cracked, was still in one piece. It looked as though it was the cover glass from a one-time lantern slide. But the most significant point of all was that the slide was divided into two sections by red and green gelatine, these being secured to the edges of the slide by transparent adhesive tape.

'I'll be darned!' ejaculated the caretaker, staring. 'How did anythin' like that ever get inside of that there door?'

'That, my friend, is a matter which calls for a deal of consideration on our part . . . and in private. All right, I have now finished with the door. Put it back again and tack the panelling back into place.'

The caretaker grunted and went to work. Meanwhile, as proud as a peacock, Carruthers studied the double-coloured slide and grinned contentedly to himself.

'Exquisite,' he murmured. 'Positively exquisite!'

'You think so?' Garth strangled a belch. 'Looks like a home-made job to me. Nothing professional about it.'

Carruthers glared. 'I'm not talking about this thing: I'm talking about my brilliance in deducing that it must be inside the door! Regarded as a work of art the thing *is* definitely crude, but it served its purpose. In another moment or two, when Atlas here has got the door back, I'll probably be able to discover how the slide was used.'

Garth swallowed a magnesia tablet, rumbled, and then stood waiting, hands deep in his overcoat pockets. Whittaker mused for a time, and then moved nearer his superior.

'I've been thinking, sir . . . '

Garth glanced. 'What brought that on?'

'About this business,' Whittaker persisted, keeping his feet solidly on the earth as usual. 'It's just got to be Cynthia Harwood, hair-do or no hair-do.'

'It has, eh? Well, now and again you come out with something which sets me thinking . . . What is it this time?'

Whittaker kept his voice down. At the moment Carruthers was out in the tunnel, taking another swig at the filth in his vacuum flask.

'For one thing she was the only one who pressed the bell. We have that from Janice Worthing and Cynthia herself. Then we have the fact that only somebody with a fair amount of money to throw about could possibly rent this basement for six months in advance. Next, money again comes into it when you think of the cost of the projector . . . Now there's another point, which I've just remembered.'

Whittaker fished his notebook from his pocket and, very deliberately thumbed through it until he came to an item.

'I have it down here, sir, from the report of the constable who was called at the very outset of this business. It says he asked Miss Harwood to ring the bell and see if it worked. It did *not* work — but no projector came into action either. Now there are two possibilities there: either she didn't push the bell button at all, or else she chose that moment to very neatly slice a penknife blade behind the bell push and cut the wires. I favour the latter notion, sir.'

'And I'll be damned if it doesn't make sense, too,' Garth admitted. 'If the rest of the trail was as clear I'd be quite happy. As it is . . . '

'Maybe it *is* clear, or at least clearer than you think. I don't want to presume in any way, sir, but as a looker-on I see most of the fight. Your ingenuity collects the evidence, but I often see a trail which you overlook.'

'Two heads better than one, eh?' Garth grinned 'Well, my lad, if you — '

'When you're ready,' Carruthers interrupted didactically. 'I didn't come here so you two could hold a whispering conference. Do you want to see how the slide works or don't you?'

Rather sheepishly Garth and Whittaker moved to where Carruthers was now standing beside the re-erected door, the caretaker having been peremptorily dispatched to his own quarters. Using his stool to give him extra height Carruthers moved the slide back and forth in the outer side of the door, the two Yard men watching him as though they expected a miracle.

'Clever!' Carruthers admitted at length. 'Have to admit that, even though not clever enough to defeat me.'

'Uh-huh,' Garth conceded foggily. 'Just the same, I don't get what you're doing.'

'You're not supposed to, yet. Give me time, can't you?'

There was another interval of fiddling, partly with the slide in the door and partly with the prepared polaroid glass. At length Carruthers stood down, closed the slide, and removed the stool.

'Now!' he exclaimed. 'This is what I think happened. We'll lose the polaroid slide inside the door again if I'm right, but Atlas can get it out again. Now, Garth, you're Janice Worthing.'

'Am I?' Garth grinned morosely. 'All right, what do I do? A can-can, or something?'

'A can't-can't would be more in your line, my unimaginative friend. To be serious again — I am Cynthia Harwood.

We have just arrived, as those two young women did on the fatal evening, and we'll construct what happened. I press the bell push — so. That doesn't mean anything with the projector disconnected, but we know what happened. Now, I draw the slide back gently, notice! *Gently!* You might check back on Janice Worthing and you'll find that Cynthia *did* move the slide gently. She dare not do anything else without wrecking the contraption. Right! So we draw it back gently. And what happens?'

'We have the polaroid slide completely in view,' Garth said, after peering at it closely.

'And the fact would not be noticed in the dim lighting of this tunnel, especially not by Janice who wasn't expecting such a thing. Okay, so they look through on to the apparent murder of Sandra Melbrane. Following me so far?'

'Completely,' Garth confirmed.

'Good! There's hope yet, then. Now, after viewing a scene as horrific as that one, what more natural than for Cynthia to slam — *slam!* — the slide back and then stand with heaving bosom and dilated eyes?'

The slide closed as Carruthers slammed the knob, from left to right. There was a faint rattling thud, then silence.

'There goes our polaroid slide inside the door,' Carruthers grinned. 'I don't suppose Janice would have noticed it. Even if she did she'd imagine it was anywhere but inside the door . . . So far so good?'

'Excellent,' Garth assented. 'Now what?'

'Now this.' Carruthers pulled the knob over again from right to left and this time it was clear glass which became visible with no sign of the polaroid slide.

'Definitely a good trick,' Garth commented. 'How's it done, anyway?'

'The polaroid slide was lying over the top of the genuine one and was slightly smaller. It was held to it by very small strips of sellotape paper — two. One at the top center and one at the bottom centre. All was well whilst the slide was moved gently, but when it was slammed back the tapes broke and deposited the polaroid slide inside the door. The main slide could not drop as well because the knob prevents it. It impales the clear slide glass to the wooden frame in which it is embedded.'

'And very nice too,' Garth commented. 'Much though I admire the way you've pulled the killer's ingenuity to pieces, Carruthers, I admire even more the mind of the killer who conceived all this in the first place.'

'Then the sooner you cease your admiration and get some action the better ... ' Carruthers paused and, surprisingly, put two fingers in his mouth and emitted a piercing whistle. In response to it the caretaker made his shuffling appearance.

'Not the door again, sir, I 'ope?' he asked anxiously.

'Just prise open the panel, that's all,' Carruthers instructed, and in about five minutes the job had been done and the polaroid slide retrieved. The treatment it had received had finished off the crack and broken the glass, but a temporary repair for the purposes of evidence could easily be effected.

'Which settles my side of the business — the mechanics thereof anyway,' Carruthers commented, putting the broken slide carefully away in the specimen box he had brought with him. 'Everything done to time, just as I'd calculated, and here is our stalwart constable back once more.'

The constable came up and saluted, casting a rather anxious look towards Garth.

'Dr. Carruthers said I could — '

'Yes, quite in order,' Garth assented. 'Carry on, constable, and I don't expect you'll be disturbed. Now, doctor, you'll want to be getting home, so — '

'Who will? I've no wife and brats chained round my neck, even if you have. The night is young yet — only half past nine. Plenty of opportunity for a conference.'

'About what?' Garth asked politely.

'You stand there and ask that with nobody charged with this diabolically clever murder? Dammit, man, if anybody needs a conference *you* do, and with somebody present to blow the fogs out of your brain.'

'All right,' Garth said gruffly. 'Let's get back to the Yard and see what's fresh.'

Carruthers collected his specimen box, stool, vacuum flask, and projector, then with his homburg on the back of his head and coat tails flying in the breeze led the way along the tunnel and ultimately to his powerful car parked near the basement area. Thereafter he drove ahead of Garth and Whittaker as they followed in the police car.

'Bang go our chances of calling this a day,' Garth sighed. 'You know what Carruthers is when he gets started: he'll be at it the rest of the night.'

'Yes, sir, that's what I'm afraid of,' Whittaker muttered. 'All very well for him: he can sleep when he wants. We've got to stick to the job.'

Garth said no more. For one thing, wind was inflating him painfully and for another he knew there was no way to sidetrack the fiendishly energetic little demon who was all too indispensable. So eventually it was a bad-tempered Garth and a pensive Whittaker who settled down in the dingy little office at the Yard,

Carruthers choosing the hide armchair and curling up in it like a gnome on a rhubarb leaf.

'Before we start,' Garth said, and reached to the intercom. 'Dick? Sling in sandwiches and coffee for three from the canteen, will you?'

'Okay, right away.'

Garth relaxed in his swivel chair, hands locked across his rumbling middle; then his eyes travelled to a report on his desk. He picked it up and read it.

'Mmm. The knife that was found by the East Division police has been sent in and examined by forensic. Tests show that the bloodstains on it tally with the blood group of Sandra. That isn't conclusive, of course, but AB being a rare group it's pretty certain it is Sandra's blood.'

'Any fingerprints?' Carruthers inquired.

'No. Dabs don't seem able to find any — at least not on the knife. Apparently they've been examining Sandra's wrap and hat to see if there are any prints on those . . . Mmm, apparently not. Hardly expected anything else. A killer as organised as this wouldn't slip up on the most vital thing of all.'

'There'll be a slip somewhere, though,' Carruthers said, with supreme confidence. 'There always is.'

Garth felt in his pocket and carefully brought his lighter to view in its chamois bag. 'At least,' he said, 'there are the prints of Cynthia's first finger and thumb on *this*. Very unorthodox, I know, since you're not supposed to fingerprint anybody until after conviction — but sometimes it's justified. This lighter is excellent for the purpose. Cleaned beforehand by the chamois leather and put back into the bag after the unwary one has supplied the prints. Cynthia fell for it completely. Take it along to C. 3, Whitty, will you? Tell Morris to get to work on it immediately, and he'd better not lose it.' He glanced at Dr. Carruthers. 'I'm assuming you might like to examine it too, doctor?'

'Right enough,' the scientist assented.

Whittaker gave his serious smile, took the lighter, and then departed. He had hardly gone before the sandwiches and

168

coffee arrived. For a while Carruthers smoked a long Russian cigarette and drank the coffee whilst Garth chewed and rumbled by turns.

'Are we decided, then, that Cynthia Harwood is the one we want?' Carruthers asked at length.

'Everything seems to point to it, certainly. Proof, though: that's the elusive quantity.'

'Suppose you stop talking round a prop and let me have the facts.'

'Very well, then. If Cynthia was responsible for the basement set-up she must also have been responsible for the murder of Sandra. Right?'

'Not necessarily. She could have worked in collusion with somebody else. *She* fixed the basement maybe — in fact certainly, as things seem at present — but somebody else polished off Sandra.'

Garth pondered this for a while and then shook his head.

'To me, Doc, it looks absolutely as though Cynthia is to blame all along. Remember, the thing that lured Sandra to her death was a phone call from a bogus

Model Salon, and it was a woman with a queer voice — or else a disguised one — who made the call ... And that reminds me,' Garth broke off, 'I've got a recording of the voice somewhere. Where the hell did I put it?'

'Be amongst the junk here somewhere,' Carruthers said. 'For the moment let it wait or you'll lose track of yourself. Up to now we believe, A, Cynthia fixed the basement. Okay. B — she may have sent the death call, since it was a woman's voice. C — well, what? Anything else to suggest Cynthia?'

'Yes, by jiminy!' Garth gave a start and lowered his coffee cup. 'Amongst so many other things I'd almost forgotten. The police surgeon's evidence is that the killer was not over-strong. Well, now, that need not so much mean a weak man as a normal woman. A woman's blow with a knife wouldn't have anything like the power of a man's.'

'Granted. And how did the police surgeon arrive at this extraordinary conclusion?'

'Something to do with the depth, or

lack of it, to which the hilt of the knife had been driven into the body.'

'C — Cynthia could have been the one who struck the blow,' Carruthers, his eyes shut over the steam of his coffee cup. 'All good leading points. What's so difficult of proof?'

'First, there's a total absence of motive — '

'Can't be. She wouldn't kill just for the fun of it, unless she's a raving maniac, and I gather she's anything but that.'

'I mean,' Garth said, glancing up briefly as Whittaker returned, 'that there's no motive I've yet been able to pin down. Maybe I will if I go to work more thoroughly on Cynthia alone. The other point is this — From two until six on the fatal day Cynthia was in a hair-do salon, having something done to her fiz-gigs under one of those space-helmet devices. She then had just time to snatch some tea, which was witnessed by the coiffurist herself, and she landed at Janice Worthing's at six-thirty. According to the surgeon, Sandra died around six-thirty also, but he is not to an hour either way because of weather conditions making it difficult to assess the state of the body.'

'Would there be anything to prevent Cynthia wiping out Sandra on her way to Janice Worthing's?'

'Yes,' Garth growled. 'The time allowed. She didn't leave the café adjoining the hairdresser's until round about six-fifteen, and it would take her quite fifteen minutes to reach Janice Worthing's even then.'

'What hairdresser's was it, and where is it situated?'

'Madame Ensard's — one of the biggest and just off Piccadilly. I didn't need to look up the address; I know it well enough already.'

'Mmm. And what time was Sandra supposed to keep her appointment?'

'Six-fifteen near McCarthy's Slag. Since she left her rooming house around six o'clock she'd just about comfortably make it to the Slag in fifteen minutes.'

'Very narrow timing, certainly,' Carruthers admitted, putting down his coffee cup. 'Forget Cynthia for the moment and see whom else we have — '

'But there *isn't* anybody else!' Garth

insisted wearily. 'The person who set the basement out must have been the killer. And it was Cynthia who did that because she operated the bell button. Besides, as we figured earlier, Whitty and I, she'd be about the only one with enough cash to swing the job.'

'That still does not prevent her working hand-in-glove with somebody else. What about Hewlett? How does he fit in?'

'He doesn't. At quarter to six on the fatal night — note the time — a customer rang up for some prints to be finished, and Hewlett tore into the job there and then and spent the evening at it.'

'Just on his say-so, I take it?'

'Naturally. I couldn't call him a liar to his face without some other evidence, could I?'

'You could, but perhaps you were frightened to do so. I am not that way given myself. What surprises me — or does it — is that you missed the most vital point of all. Find out from this supposed customer if he *did* ring up for his prints. If he *did*, then all things being equal, it's possible that Hewlett may be speaking the truth.'

'Mmm.' Garth thumped his chest and then glanced towards Whittaker. 'Get Hewlett at his home, Whitty, if he's there — and if he isn't, tell his folks to have him ring me the moment he comes in.'

Whittaker nodded, flipped through the directory, and presently picked up the 'phone. Garth was by now studying another report, which said quite briefly that all attempts to discover information concerning anybody in the region of McCarthy's Slag had ended in failure. Carruthers, for his part, looked as if he were asleep, his half consumed Russian cigarette smouldering between his acid-stained fingers.

'Hewlett, sir,' Whittaker said finally, handing the phone across. 'He's in, fortunately.'

'Fortunately, he's in,' Carruthers corrected with a growl. 'For God's sake talk English, lad!'

Whittaker remained quite composed and waited as Garth took the phone.

'Hewlett? Garth here. I'm checking up. Let me have the address of that customer who wanted his prints in a hurry, will you? And obviously it's no use your saying you don't know it.'

'Of course I know it,' came Terry's voice. 'Michael Ealing, 'The Willows,' Malborough Crescent, W.C. Can I ask why you want to know?'

'Just checking up.' Garth scribbled the address down. 'And on the night Sandra died this individual rang you up at quarter to six and asked for his prints, which you finished during the evening?'

'Yes. There were four hundred of them — a man-sized commercial job that took me a whole evening to complete. Contact printing, that is.'

'Much obliged,' Garth said brusquely. ''Bye.'

He put the receiver back and glanced at Whittaker. Not that Whittaker needed instructions, since he was already looking through the telephone directory.

'Two numbers, sir,' he said at length. 'Works, and residence. Shall I try the residence?'

'If you will.' Garth finished off his sandwiches and coffee whilst he was waiting, then took the 'phone Whittaker handed to him. At the end of three minutes questions and answers he knew exactly where he stood.

'Everything as Hewlett said,' he sighed, looking at Carruthers. 'As watertight as Cynthia's. The customer *did* ring, and Hewlett was engaged on . . . '

'Yes, yes, I gathered that,' Carruthers broke in impatiently. 'No need to stress the obvious, man. It is conceivable, of course, that Hewlett could have slipped out long enough to put an end to Sandra, but that doesn't link up too well with the timing. No, he doesn't *fit* somehow.'

'No more than Cynthia does,' Garth sighed. 'I'll begin to think in a bit that maybe Janice Worthing had something to do with it, but since she didn't operate the bell push at any time, that is ruled out. No, it's Cynthia. But how, when, where?'

'To have planned this murder,' Whittaker said absently, 'Cynthia must at some stage have seen the film whereby to create the basement illusion, and according to our records, sir, there was not time

176

when she *did* see it. Apparently she did not see it when Hewlett processed it, nor when Kindross had it.'

'True . . . ' Garth sat scowling, dragging a cheroot from his case meanwhile; then a sudden thought seemed to strike him. Getting to his feet he went over to the nearby steel cupboard and from it took the diary he had appropriated from Sandra's flat. Coming back to the desk he threw himself in the swivel chair and flicked the diary's pages swiftly.

'What now?' Carruthers asked, obviously bored.

'It occurs to me,' Garth answered, 'that since Sandra made a note of keeping the appointment for the film murder scene, she may refer to it again later on. I didn't look that far. Somehow, no matter how indirect the clue, we might gain some information about Cynthia, and then we — '

Garth stopped, stared at a page of the diary, then snapped his fingers.

'Corn in Egypt!' he exclaimed. 'Listen to this — It's an entry for — er — a week before Sandra was murdered. 'Saw Cyn

Harwood today and told her about my murder act for amateur film for Arthur Kindross. She seemed unusually interested since as a rule I have the impression she isn't much interested in filming.'

'Handy things, diaries,' Carruthers murmured. 'Just as long as no flatfoot gets hold of mine. I'd be had for libel if that happened.'

'This,' Garth said, slapping the diary down on the desk, 'is something worth knowing. Cynthia knew about the film through Sandra herself. Though it doesn't say so here we can be pretty sure that she'd pump Sandra dry of information concerning it.'

'Which gets us where, sir?' Whittaker asked, pondering.

Garth did not answer for a moment. He reflected, his eyes on distance, then finally he whipped up the telephone.

'Riverside 2910,' he said curtly; and after a moment or two: 'Mr. Kindross? Garth here again, and I apologise for my lateness in calling. Regarding that 3-d film which Sandra Melbrane featured in. Where is the film now?'

'In its can in my den — or rather studio. I've got a small room I keep by specially for photography.'

'But you surely didn't take that film just for your own amusement?'

'Not at all. I'm entering it later in a competition.'

'I'd like to be assured that the film is still there to *be* entered! When did you last see it in this den of yours?'

'On the night my wife and I had a look at it . . . ' There was an odd hesitation in Kindross's voice. 'Just a moment: I'll check up on it.'

Garth relaxed, smiling rather tautly to himself. His smile became even wider when Kindross spoke again.

'The damned thing's gone! I've not the least idea when, or where to! My wife doesn't know a thing about it.'

'Did you keep it in any special box, or anything?'

'Lord, no! I didn't consider it *that* valuable. I just put it down on the bench alongside the projector, camera, and all the rest of my photographic tackle. That's the odd thing: the valuable stuff isn't touched, yet the film's disappeared.'

'I rather thought it might have,' Garth said dryly.

'Don't touch anything, Mr. Kindross. I'm sending round a couple of men, late though it is, to examine your den thoroughly. There may be useful finger-prints or some kind of clue that will help us. Believe me, the theft of that film is linked up with the murder of Sandra Melbrane. 'Bye for now.'

Garth dropped the 'phone back to its cradle and rubbed his thick hands.

'You heard that, gentlemen?'

'Distinctly,' Carruthers acknowledged. 'The inference being that Cynthia Har-wood, having got all the facts from Sandra, made it her business to appropri-ate the film — or else paid some person of a burgling frame of mind to do it for her.'

'Right!' Garth glanced at Whittaker. 'On your way to Kindross, Whitty, and see what you can dig up. Take Matthews with you in case there should be fingerprints.'

'Yes, sir,' Whittaker assented, and

glanced towards the clock. The time was not very far from eleven.

'Bit by bit,' Garth murmured. 'Even when you're reasonably sure who's guilty it's the devil's own job to pin it down. I suppose I could take out a search warrant and have Cynthia's place ransacked for evidence, only I doubt if it would do any good. She'll have taken good care to get rid of everything suspicious. It would also make her realize that we're on to her and that could delay our nailing her.'

'Umph,' Carruthers agreed, his eyes shut as he appeared to be dozing in the armchair.

'Also,' Garth continued, 'I've just realised something else. The reason for finding the knife and wrap so near to the actual scene of the crime. Cynthia must have committed the murder a little while before driving on to Janice Worthing's. She could hardly take the knife with her, could she, in case it happened to be seen? And the wrap would be a bulky problem — Quite normal, therefore, to bury both on the Slag and leave it at that.'

Carruthers opened his eyes abruptly.

'Let me see that report from Dabs, will you?'

Garth handed it over, looking vaguely surprised. Carruthers read the report through, his lips jutting arrogantly.

'Who made the analysis on the knife, anyway?' he demanded. 'What the devil is this signature supposed to be?'

'Robert Hilton. He's one of the junior men — '

'I can believe it, and I'll wager he's missed something too. Listen, Garth, here's an angle . . . Doing the things she did, Cynthia would get either her hands or her gloves dirty, would she not? Now — unless she had the foresight to think of two pairs of gloves, which I hope she didn't — she'd never turn up at Janice's with dirty gloves, because that would be a complete give-away — and yet Sandra's body was half buried in cinders and dirt and so were the knife and wrap. I'll gamble that Cynthia took her gloves *off* after the killing, while she did the really dirty work, then put them on again when she went to Janice's. I expect, too, she'd keep them on when wielding the knife for the death blow. But would she be so careful in regard to the wrap when she buried it?'

'It's certainly an angle,' Garth admitted — and Carruthers picked up the report again.

'I notice that the wrap and knife are lumped together under one analyzed heading. Cynthia might not think that fingerprints would show on the wrap, though she'd be careful regarding the knife. In other words, barring two pairs of gloves, there is the chance that fingerprints may be on the wrap.'

'But they aren't!' Garth objected. 'The report says so.'

'With all due respect to your backroom boys,' Carruthers sneered, 'I have more often found them slipping up on their analyses than being thorough. Routine jobs often don't give a good result. Give me that wrap and with my apparatus, using infra-red photography, I'll find the vaguest suggestion of a whorl, arch, or loop if it's there to be found.'

'Knife, too?'

'No — tie your exhibit label on that

and put it away. Cynthia would make no mistake there.'

'And if Cynthia washed her hands before reaching Janice's? She *could*, you know.'

Carruthers grinned. 'With time so short? Have you ever reckoned how long it takes a fastidious woman to freshen up after a job as messy as that?'

'Mmm — I see what you mean. Right, I'll see you have the wrap before you leave.'

'Now,' Carruthers said, apparently as fresh as though he had just arisen from a long sleep, 'you can let me hear that tape recording you brought from Sandra's rooming house.'

Garth sighed and glanced meaningfully at the clock. As far as he could see, the present conference could easily be carried on next day, since there was no likelihood of Cynthia being aware of a net tightening gradually around her. Carruthers, though, was evidently on the crest of one of his inspirational waves, and nothing else but definite action would satisfy him.

Garth found the tape spool amidst the

papers on his desk and took it across to the nearby recorder. Switching it on he stood and watched the effect on Carruthers as, another Russian cigarette in his lips, he listened drowsily.

'Sounds disguised somehow, to me,' Garth said, when the recording had run through. 'What's your opinion?'

'The person concerned is using the normal voice but is speaking into a cocoa tin, or something like it. An empty one, of course. That produces a resonance and so distorts the voice that the ear cannot recognise it as belonging to anybody in particular.'

'Which is a great big help to us.'

'The ear,' Carruthers said, 'is the most fallible of all human senses, especially when it comes to a case as vital as this. Scientific instruments, however, can overcome the fallibility of the ear. What must be done with that recording is to have it photographed.'

'You mean the spool?' Garth was looking hazy.

'No, *no!* I mean photograph the voice as it speaks, transform it into optical sound, just the same as a track on the edge of a film. That is optical sound, visible as peaks and valleys.'

'And what good will that do?'

'It will show the peaks and valleys distinctly, and all the cocoa tins on earth cannot distort those peaks at the maximum or the valleys at the minimum. The sound *as* sound is most deceptive, but when you see the sound, so to speak, it's a different story. Every voice, Garth, is different, as individual as fingerprints, and no two voices are identical in the peak and valley reading. So, I'll photograph this sound recording on to a visual track and then we'll somehow trick Cynthia into speaking normally to us and convert *that* into a visual track. If she spoke in the first instance the peak and valley maximum and minimum will absolutely match, and no disguising will alter it. Disguised or otherwise a voice can only reach a certain *natural* pitch, and that is what visual sound records.'

'Masterly!' Garth murmured, and then spoiled his praise by belching with startling force.

'Thank you for the compliment — thunder included,' Carruthers snorted. 'It's as I've said all along, Garth, these fools who think they can literally get away with murder fail to realise that modern science is always one jump ahead. In a few more years crime will, I believe, be impossible because an electronic brain will be able to solve the problem by just being placed on the scene of the crime . . . Matter of fact, I'm working on a machine of that type right now.'

'Good,' Garth murmured absently. Then, 'Motive! What the blazes was Cynthia's motive behind all this brilliant twisting and turning? I can make several guesses, but I've got to be sure.'

'It'll drop into place with the rest of the stuff,' the little scientist said complacently. 'And now there is something else . . .'

7

Garth brought the tape spool across to his desk and looked at the diminutive scientist inquiringly.

'*Plenty* else, I'd say!'

'It concerns Sandra's body.' Carruthers' keen eyes were abstracted. 'The surgeon places her death at six-thirty, and is not sure of it. For myself, I don't think he's very far wrong, though I'd say thirty minutes either way is permissible. Now, she left her flat at six o'clock. Right?'

'That's correct,' Garth assented.

'And for reasons which we already know she was dressed in her amethyst evening gown. That would show below the wrap she was wearing and identify her immediately. The street lights would be bright enough near her flat for that?'

'Quite bright enough,' Garth admitted.

'Mmm . . . ' Carruthers blew a smoke ring and pondered. 'And what time did Cynthia come out of the hairdressers and go into the café?'

'Well, she didn't give me the exact spot-on time, but I'd say it must have been between quarter to six and quarter past.'

'And what kind of a car has Cynthia?'

'It's one of those small but powerful racing types.'

'Right. Let's assume that Cynthia went into the café around quarter to six and stayed a few minutes, leaving maybe at five to six. In twenty minutes she could easily reach the Slag — or rather those two streets you referred to — and commit the crime. Sandra would be there by then, identifiable by her long evening gown and wrap. Earlier I'd thought of Cynthia maybe picking her up at her flat, but that timing doesn't fit. No — the other course is the most logical. Have you questioned Madame Ensard yet concerning Cynthia?'

'Had no time.'

'Then do it now. Madam Ensard is well known enough: she'll be on the phone at home. If you wake her out of her beauty sleep it can't be helped.'

Garth shrugged, smothered a yawn,

and picked up the directory. When he had the number he dialled it. The voice of a maid replied.

'Madame is just about to retire,' she said.

'And so are you probably,' Garth sympathised. 'Sorry, but I must speak to her. This is urgent.'

Long pause and then an irritable woman's voice.

'Yes, yes, what is it? Madame Ensard speaking.'

'My apologies, madam, for the late call, but this is Chief Inspector Garth, C.I.D. Two days ago I believe you had a lady by the name of Miss Harwood at your salon for some hair titivation or other?'

'Oh, yes, indeed! Miss Harwood! She is a very good friend and client of mine.'

'Splendid! How long did her hair-do take?'

'Three to four hours. It is a long process.'

'I believe she had tea in your attached caféteria and that you saw her there?'

'I did, yes.'

'Can you recall what time she left? It is

most important.'

'Yes, it was twenty past six — '

'Twenty past six?' Garth interrupted, frowning. 'What makes you so sure of that?'

'Well, I had tea at the same table as Miss Harwood. I remember she glanced at the clock, saw it was twenty past six, and then said something about having an urgent appointment. She checked the time by her watch, which was also at twenty past six — and then she left as quickly as possible.'

'I . . . see.' Garth dragged the two words out as though he did not know what to make of the situation — which indeed he did not, at that moment.

'Will there be anything else?' Madame Ensard asked, after a moment, and Garth gave a start.

'Er — no, madam, thank you. Tomorrow I'll probably look in at your establishment. I'd rather like to see the caféteria for myself.'

'By all means, inspector. I'll be there all day. Goodbye.'

Garth put the phone down and glanced

across at Carruthers. He gave a shrug.

'I heard her clearly enough. The one thing emerging from it is that Cynthia could never have done anything to Sandra if she didn't leave that cafeteria until six-twenty.'

'No *if* about it, Carruthers.'

'I'm not so sure. I very much doubt, at that late time, if she could even reach Janice Worthing's by six-thirty, but apparently she did. Well, maybe the cafeteria itself will show us something. I'll come along with you tomorrow. What time? Around ten?'

'Uh-huh, about then.' Then, as Carruthers got to his feet, 'You'll be wanting that wrap from the fingerprint department — '

'And that lighter of yours for comparison prints, if you please.'

Garth nodded. 'I leave the sound into vision trick to you, then, along with this fingerprinting?'

'Naturally. By tomorrow morning I'll probably have an interesting statement to make.'

Garth paused at the office door. 'So soon?'

'Certainly! You don't imagine I'm going to spend the night sleeping when there are more important things to do, do you?'

* * *

Garth arrived at his office an hour earlier than usual the following morning — namely nine o'clock. To his satisfaction — not to say surprise — Whittaker was already there, arranging the day's correspondence and messages into orderly files.

'Morning, Whitty.' Garth hung up his hat and coat. 'How did you get on last night at Kindross's? Anything interesting?'

'No fingerprints, sir, I regret to say. Plenty of smudges, according to Matthews, which don't get us anywhere. It was perfectly obvious that the thing was a burglary done by somebody who's quite an amateur. Pantry window had been forced, and after that the prowler must have crept around until she, if it was Cynthia, found the right place. Be in the night, I suppose, when Kindross and his wife were asleep.'

'Mmm.' Garth massaged his chest and pondered. 'And that's the best there is?'

'There's this, sir. May be useful.'

Whittaker held out a cellophane envelope and at first sight it appeared to be empty, then when he came to look more closely Garth realised that there was a solitary hair inside — long, dark, and with a slight curl.

'Where did this come from?' Garth asked abruptly.

'I found it caught in the wood at the top of the pantry window frame. The only person who could possibly have left it there was somebody who climbed through the window. It does not belong to either Kindross or his wife: they're both blonde.'

'Good! Take it to forensic afterwards and tell 'em to hang on to it until further notice. They can get it mounted meanwhile. We're going to grab a hair from Cynthia if it kills us. Forensic will do the rest.'

'Without her guessing what you're up to?' Whittaker asked dubiously.

'Yes — we're going to try a little

strategy. I'm going to ring up Cynthia in a moment and get her to come over here right away. She can be here before Carruthers arrives at ten.'

'Oh! He's coming again, then?'

'Definitely — and with useful information, I hope. Ten o'clock, he said. When Cynthia arrives, Whitty, hop along to the photographic department and get a small bowl full of hyposulphate crystals. Bring them in as part of an important case and hand them to me across Cynthia's head. She'll be seated, of course. I'll do the rest. At the same time we'll take a recording of the conversation, then Carruthers can do a sound-to-vision act whenever he wishes.'

Whittaker nodded vaguely. Since he had not been present when Carruthers had given his sound-to-vision theory the previous night he could not be blamed for looking bewildered. Nor did Garth think of explaining further. He reached to the telephone and yanked it up, then remembered the directory and quickly thumbed through it to Cynthia's number.

'Good morning, inspector,' came her

serene voice, as at length Garth contacted her.

'Glad to catch you in, Miss Harwood.'

'Little reason to go out in such dirty weather, inspector. More information wanted?'

'Matter of fact there is, but I can't spare the time to come over and see you. I must ask you to come to my office right away. Within the next half hour.'

'Certainly, if you wish it. See you later.'

The line clicked and Garth grinned. He sat back in the swivel chair and rubbed his hands.

'Up to now all's well. She'll be here — and I'd better bring you up to date, Whitty, on the information you missed last night.'

'Thank you, sir. I'd be glad of it.'

So Garth lighted a cheroot and then went into the details. Whittaker listened attentively, his brow creased as he came to the problem of 'six-twenty.'

'Afraid I don't understand that bit at all, sir.' he confessed. 'Cynthia couldn't have done it in the time. I'd say that maybe there was some juggling with the clock, only Madame Ensard would surely have her own watch with which to make a check, apart from Cynthia? No, it's got me stopped. Maybe we're not looking for Cynthia at all.'

'Oh, yes we are,' Garth declared flatly, his cheroot at an acute angle. 'It just can't be anybody else now because all the other factors have been eliminated. It's a matter of *how* she did and *why* she did it. We'll trip her up soon, somehow.'

Whittaker nodded, prepared to leave it at that, then picking up the hair in its envelope he left the office en route for forensic. Garth meanwhile busied himself with the tape recorder, setting the microphone volume control and placing the foot pedal remote control beside his desk . . . After which, even when Whittaker had returned, there was nothing to do but wait.

And towards quarter to ten Cynthia arrived, immaculately dressed, quite composed.

'Ah, good morning, Miss Harwood!' Garth appeared to be all geniality as he shook hands. 'Sorry to have to drag you out like this.'

'That's all right. Doesn't take long in my car. It's pretty fast, you know.'

'Yes, so I imagine.' Garth exchanged an unnoticed glance with Whittaker and drew up a chair for the girl to seat herself. Removing her gloves she sat playing with them gently as Garth went back to his swivel chair and, true to orders, Whittaker absented himself. Garth touched the foot control of the tape recorder and then examined the glowing end of his cheroot.

'Matter of fact, Miss Harwood, I just wanted to ask you again about the hairdressers. You said Madame Ensard, did you not?'

'That is correct, yes.'

'My main concern is the time you left. I have checked back with Madame Ensard — purely routine, you understand — and she tells me you left at twenty past six, consulting both the caféteria clock, and your watch.'

'I did just that, certainly, and it *was* twenty past six.'

'And Madame confirmed the time also?' Garth's cold eyes never left the girl's face.

'Well, no. She doesn't wear a watch.'

'She doesn't?' Garth looked astonished. 'How extraordinary for a woman in her position.'

Cynthia smiled, with the slightest shade of uneasiness. 'She told me once when a question of the right time arose that she never wears her watch whilst in the salon because steam-heat and chemicals affect it.'

'Ah, I see — quite understandable. And when did she tell you this?'

'Quite some while ago. I can't remember exactly.'

Garth pressed a bell push under the desk edge and sat back.

'You certainly must have cut the time very fine to reach Mrs. Worthing's for six-thirty and arrive, so I understand, all neat and tidy.'

'My car broke the speed limit, I'm afraid — or shouldn't I say that to a chief inspector?'

Garth grinned. 'I am not a traffic cop, Miss Harwood: My main concern is murder and the perpetrators thereof. Yes, sergeant, what is it?' he asked formally, as Whittaker tapped and came in.

'Sorry to interrupt, sir, but this matter's in urgent need of settlement ... ' Whittaker held up a small glass bowl of crystals resembling soda.

'Oh, yes, the Barker case,' Garth assented blandly. 'Forgive me a moment, Miss Harwood — Let me have the bowl, sergeant.'

Whittaker handed it straight across Cynthia's head and Garth took good care to muff the job. Several of the crystals tipped out on to the girl's hat and into her hair. Immediately she stirred uneasily.

'Keep quite still, madam,' Garth said quickly. 'If any of these crystals get near your eyes they may cause trouble. As it is, you're still safe. You're a damned clumsy idiot, sergeant! Why can't you be more careful?'

'Sorry, sir,' Whittaker mumbled.

'Don't just stand there!' Cynthia cried angrily, holding herself rigid. 'Get the beastly stuff out of the way, whatever it is!'

'Those forceps!' Garth ordered. 'Quickly!'

Whittaker handed them over and very carefully Garth picked the harmless crystals up one by one and restored them to the bowl, finally handing the forceps back to Whittaker with one or two dark hairs trapped within them.

'Take the stuff back to forensic!' Garth snapped. 'I've no time to bother with it now — and next time watch what you're doing!'

Whittaker went out and Cynthia rolled her dark eyes upwards.

'Can I move?' she demanded.

'Yes, of course. I really am sorry, madam. A complete accident, I assure you. I'm afraid your coiffure is considerably disarranged.'

Cynthia whipped a compact from her bag and stared at her reflection crossly.

'Disarranged is right! I've a good mind to bring an action against the C.I.D. for this! What's more, I *will* if I find I'm burned or singed anywhere . . . '

'I don't think you'll find anything like that, madam. Anyhow, I won't detain you any longer: you'll want to straighten up, I'm sure. I'll probably ring you later.'

'Very well!' Cynthia glared, ignored Garth's proffered hand, then swept out of the office. He grinned thoughtfully to himself and crushed the stub of his cheroot in the ashtray.

'Mmm — so the imperturbable young lady has a nasty temper, has she? Quite a revelation — and unasked for, too.'

The door clicked and Whittaker returned. He gave his reserved smile.

'We managed that very nicely, sir. Forensic are checking on the hairs now. They'll have something pretty quickly.'

'Good enough,' Garth nodded, returning to his chair. 'I also had the unique opportunity of seeing our lady friend's behaviour when 'caught out.' She's got the nastiest temper imaginable. Evidently all that suavity of hers is just stuck on.'

'Evidently, sir I — '

'So you're here, are you?' Carruthers came through the still open doorway, homburg on the back of his head and an infuriating smile on his powerful mouth.

'Where did you expect we'd be?' Garth asked sourly. 'On the roof?'

'No — in bed, or eating. No wonder you have dyspepsia, Garth. Oh, sergeant, there's a sound-projector in my car. Fetch it up for me, will you? I'm not so tough as I look.'

Whittaker failed completely to grasp this last crack, but left the office just the same. Garth stood expectantly by his swivel chair and gave his chest a savage bang.

'Get anywhere?' he asked, as the little scientist tossed down Sandra's wrap and then from his capacious overcoat brought forth the reel of recording tape and cigarette lighter.

'That,' Carruthers said, 'is a dangerous question to ask of a man like me! Of *course* I got somewhere! My guess that there might be a print somewhere on the wrap proved correct, but it took infra-red equipment to locate it. Here — take a look at these.'

Garth took a photographic print from Carruthers' hand and studied it intently. It was divided into two sections so that a thumb print was visible, bisected neatly down the middle.

'Nice piece of dactylography, don't you think?' Carruthers asked. 'Notice the whorl and ridge characteristics. Since in law there must be sixteen identical characteristics in two prints, I think we can say this qualifies. There are eighteen, as a matter of fact. That isn't one print divided down the centre: it comprises two! Half is from the cigarette lighter thumb print, and the other half from the one clear print in the lining of the wrap. Conclusive enough.'

Garth nodded grimly. 'Cynthia's the one we want; that's settled.'

'In regard to the voice, I've transformed the track into visual sound but I'll need a matching track of Cynthia's normal voice before I do anything.'

'Right here.' Garth lifted the loaded spool from the tape recorder. 'I had her here before you came, and took her voice without her knowledge. Also some of her hair, again without her knowledge.'

'Hair?' Carruthers looked surprised until Garth explained, by which time Whittaker had arrived with the heavy sound-projector. He put it carefully in a corner and waited for the next instruction.

'Madame Ensard is our next stop,' Garth said. 'If you're ready, Carruthers?'

'I'm *always* ready. It's you fellows who lag behind. We can use my car. Faster than that mass production job you crawl around in.'

Garth and Whittaker glanced at each other as they followed Carruthers from the office, but they did not pass any comment. The ex-boffin was evidently in one of his most sarcastic moods so the best thing was to humour him.

'I've given quite a bit of thought to this twenty past six angle,' Carruthers said, as he drove at hair-raising speed amidst the city traffic, 'and there's only one possible answer.'

'What?' Garth asked, wincing as daggers went through his midriff.

'She must have had an opportunity somewhere to put the clock forward, and to advance her own watch to match it would be an easy job. Bit of a mystery why Madame herself didn't spot the flaw, though.'

'That bit bothered me,' Garth admitted, 'but Cynthia let it drop this morning that Madame never wears a watch in the salon because of steam and what-have-you. She *also* let it drop that she'd known that for some time — so in planning ahead she could be pretty sure that Madame would not be able to check the time there and then, and probably wouldn't bother to later on in any case.'

'Very nice,' Carruthers approved. 'And incidentally, where exactly is this hair-dresser's, anyway?'

'Keep going,' Garth directed. 'I'll show you.'

Which he did, quite successfully, and towards ten-fifteen he, Carruthers, and Whittaker were amidst the smell of perfume and surrounded by slinky love-lies who looked at them curiously.

'Madame Ensard, if you please,' Garth requested gruffly, feeling thoroughly uncomfortable amidst so much feminine pulchritude. 'The name's Garth — C.I.D.'

The flutter that began in the dove-cote ended as Madame appeared. She was short, grossly fat, yet somehow interesting.

'Just a matter of us looking around, Madame,' Garth explained, after the formality of exhibiting his warrant card. 'These two gentlemen are with me. The caféteria is our main objective.'

'Yes, of course . . . ' Madame led the way from the salon entrance into a long, cold corridor — then a thought seemed to strike her. She stopped and turned. 'By the way, inspector, I think there is something you ought to know. I'd have told you last night, only the discovery was not made until this morning. The caféteria clock, you know . . . '

'Yes?' Garth asked keenly, 'What about it?'

'Ever since the day when Miss Harwood was here the clock has been gaining incredibly! Not that *she* had anything to do with it, naturally, but your mentioning twenty past six as the time she left, makes me instance her. It must have been gaining then, also. We've found the reason now, and put it right — or rather my man-of-all-work did.'

'And what *was* the reason?' Garth asked patiently.

'Well, extraordinarily enough, somebody had tightened up the screw on the pendulum, making it swing at double its normal speed, thereby causing a tremendous gain. It's a wall clock, you know,

with the pendulum visible through a little glass opening.'

'I see,' Garth nodded, with a significant glance at Carruthers and Whittaker. 'Tell me, Madame, is the caféteria open all the time your salon is?'

'Only in summer. At this time of year I have it opened around three — '

'Then anybody could get into it even though they would not be served with anything?'

'Of course — but my dear inspector, who would *want* to?'

'I can think of one person,' Garth smiled. 'However, let it pass. I don't think we'll need to see the caféteria, Madame. You have told us quite enough.'

'I have?' The hair stylist seemed completely at sea, and Garth did not take the trouble to enlighten her. Indeed he could not, without mentioning names, so he excused himself as politely as possible and led the way back to Carruthers' parked car.

'Still more ingenuity,' Garth commented. 'Cynthia must have known all about the caféteria hours and about the

clock being of the pendulum variety. All she had to do was slip out and tighten the pendulum screw — or what is more likely is that she did it on entering the salon, before having her hair fixed. That would give the clock a longer time in which to gain. She was smart enough not to actually alter the time by a twenty minute jump or something in case it had been noticed by somebody a little while before she tampered with it. I observed the ladies' cloakroom just beside the caféteria door, so she had ample opportunity to disappear in that direction before getting her hair fixed. After that, to fix her own watch to match would be a trifle.'

'That young woman,' Carruthers said, musing, 'is brilliant enough to be my daughter. But thank God she isn't — Well, back to the Yard, I take it?'

'That's up to you,' Garth said. 'What about making a visual of Cynthia's office recording?'

'The recording is still in your office: I didn't bring it with me. Besides, you've some messing about to finish with some hairs, haven't you?'

'Mmm, yes,' Garth admitted. 'If they've done it yet — Right, doc, if you don't mind. Back to the Yard.'

Carruthers murmured something about not being a 'damned chauffeur' and set his powerful car in motion. Once back at the Yard Garth wasted no time in heading for the forensic department, where Phillips, the day technician in charge, was personally working on the hair problem. He had both of them embedded like nearly invisible needles in a base of Friar's Balsam, upon which was trained the ruthless eye of an electron microscope.

'Well?' Garth asked him, as Carruthers looked on with a rather pitying smile. 'How are you making out?'

'Just about finished, chief. The curl index, pigmentation, and medulla check exactly. Around sixty microns, which means it is head hair and from the length of it, a woman's — else a man in pretty poor condition with very long hair.'

'It's a woman's,' Garth said quietly, and gave his chest a grand slam. 'You mean they both agree?'

'They're from the same person, definitely. One is the specimen Whittaker here brought in early on: the other is from the batch of 'em, nearly half a dozen, which were clamped in a pair of forceps.'

'Thanks,' Garth said quietly. 'Make out your report and let me have it, will you, in readiness for the evidence.'

'Okay . . . '

Pondering, Garth led the way out of the laboratory, and all three were back in the office before he spoke again.

'Funny thing,' he muttered, lighting one of his eternal weeds, 'but I always feel pretty foul when I know I've caught somebody in the net — that I'm within an ace of dealing the sledge-hammer blow. Maybe I'm too soft-hearted to be in this business.'

'Stop drivelling and let's finish the job,' Carruthers said curtly. 'If you catch yourself getting sentimental just think how the victim must have felt in the last moments at the hands of the killer. *That's* the angle that matters, and the destruction of an assassin, be it man or woman, is only common sense. Right! Now about this voice recording . . . you'd better see it. Mmm.'

Carruthers stopped and thought, then sighed. 'Come to think of it, it would be better if we did this in my own laboratory. Seeing this recording by itself doesn't mean anything. We need the companion to it — Cynthia's own natural voice — and see if it matches. Sorry, Whittaker — you'll have to take the projector down to my car again, if you don't mind.'

'Not at all,' Whittaker growled, and lugged the heavy apparatus out of the office, Garth and Carruthers following behind him . . .

After which there was a fair journey by road to be made to Carruthers' home. It was towards noon when the trip was completed, but evidently the little scientist had anticipated everything, for his housekeeper had prepared an excellent lunch for three. This completed, retirement was made to the laboratory — that amazing area of instruments and queer gadgets that were quite beyond the comprehension of the two Yard men.

'Whatever you do, don't interrupt me,'

Carruthers ordered. 'If you do, I may make that rare thing — a mistake.'

With that, he scrambled into his stained and somewhat tattered overall and began work. To Whittaker it was fascinating. To Garth, already getting the rebound from his lunch, it was tedious. He hung around, smoked interminably, and listened to the recorded voice of Cynthia chattering forth, together with his own and Whittaker's remarks. Finally, it was towards half past three — six cups of weak tea later — when Carruthers removed a length of film from a drying rack and studied it carefully.

'Exquisite!' he exclaimed. 'A real Carruthers job! Now for the vital test of matching. First, you can see how the sound looks visually. Whether you're interested or not doesn't matter — I am! Now, let's see.'

He threaded up the film in the projector and then closed the shutters over the windows. Blank darkness fell, to very soon be alleviated by the appearance on a screen, at the far end of the laboratory, of dancing lines and dagger points which leapt in and out.

'Sound track — nothing more,' Carruthers explained, and then switched on the photo-electric equipment to provide the matching voice that exactly synchronised with the jumping lines on the screen. The whole thing was a transcription in light and sound of the original message sent to Sandra.

'Okay so far,' Carruthers said, opening one of the shutters. 'Now let's try a bit of matching.'

Abandoning the projector he turned to an object like an old-time magic lantern — plainly a slide-projector fitted with a dual gate. Into this he threaded the two films — the one the message on the phone, and the other Cynthia's voice in the office. When he switched on there appeared two sets of zig-zag lines, across the sides and top of which were ruled scales. The whole projection looked exactly like a seismograph record, or else a bad drawing of the Himalayas.

'Watch!' Carruthers commanded, and twiddled a knob. In response to this the two zig-zag lines moved separately, their images turned horizontal by means of prisms . . . Garth and Whittaker watched intently, their eyes on one 'peak' which exactly touched the '120' line. After a good deal of adjustment Carruthers finally succeeded in getting the lower zig-zag peaks to also reach the '120' line. This done he gave a deep sigh of contentment.

'That's it!' he said. 'Conclusive! On the top half you have the highest normal note possible in the voice that spoke on the 'phone. In the lower half you have the same peak again, spoken in the *natural* voice. As unerringly as a spectrograph gives the constitution of a metal, so this proves both voices to belong to the same person.'

There was silence for a moment, then the shutters swung open again. Carruthers stood with his hands plunged in his overall pockets, musing. Finally he looked at Garth.

'All yours now, Garth,' he said, shrugging. 'My part's done, and all this evidence will stand in a court of law. Cynthia Harwood is the culprit. Inch by inch, between us, we've pulled every move she'd made completely apart. We've got everything.'

'Except motive,' Garth muttered. 'Maybe she'll explain that when we reach her. Thanks for all you've done, doc. We'll be on our way back to the Yard. There's a warrant to be made out for Cynthia's arrest.'

This technicality was not a matter that took very long, and towards five o'clock Whittaker drew up the patrol car outside Cynthia's home. As before, they were conducted into the lounge, and presently Cynthia came in to them.

'Again, gentlemen?' She looked surprised. 'I'm commencing to feel quite flattered by your attentions!'

Garth remained solemn. 'Cynthia Harwood, I have here a warrant for your arrest, and I charge you that you did, on the date of January tenth last, murder one Sandra Melbrane. It is my duty to warn you that anything you may say will be taken down and may be used as evidence at your trial.'

'Is this a joke?' Cynthia asked bitterly.

For answer Garth held forth the warrant. She stared at it; then suddenly the calm complacency left her face. Fright came into it instead and the colour vanished from her cheeks.

'It's — it's a lot of trumped-up rubbish!' she declared huskily.

'On the contrary, Miss Harwood.' Garth shook his head and Whittaker phlegmatically made notes. 'Every move you have made has been scientifically worked out — from the very moment when you first heard of the cine film murder from Sandra, and from that point onwards conceived the killing of Sandra by means of photographic illusions, accelerated clocks, and even the theft of the film itself from Kindross.'

'You've no proof!' Cynthia panted. 'You can't have!'

Garth looked at her fixedly. 'Madam, we have *infallible* proof. The scientific matching of your voice for one thing — since you made the phone appointment that lured Sandra to her death. We have matched specimens of your hair from the pantry window in Kindross's home; matched thumb prints which you left on Sandra's wrap ... The trap has closed, Miss Harwood. I must ask you to get your things and come with us. The car is waiting.'

Cynthia hesitated, then she suddenly laughed bitterly. 'Serves me right, I suppose! And I was sure I did it so perfectly and didn't leave a clue!'

Whittaker scribbled hastily in short-hand and Garth remained stonily attentive.

'The rent of that basement paid anonymously; the trade plate made by the same process. The investigation I had to go through in secret! I couldn't have managed it if that old fool of a caretaker hadn't been so short-sighted. He never even spotted me in my early investigations. I'm telling you all this!' she shouted abruptly. 'You're probably wondering why?'

Garth shrugged. 'Quite immaterial. We have our evidence. If you wish to verify it, all the better.'

'I'm not verifying anything!' Cynthia was suddenly defiant, plainly too confused in thought to realise what she *was* saying. 'I put it to you, as two decent men — for I suppose you're that in spite of being hounds of the law — what would *you* do if you saw the man you loved being dragged down into dishonour and heaven knows what immorality by an utterly unscrupulous woman?'

Garth smiled coldly. 'You'd better think things out a little more carefully, Miss Harwood. You are apparently trying to convey the impression that you murdered Miss Melbrane because she was entangling Mr. Hewlett. That cannot be true because all through you have tried to shift the blame to Hewlett, even to taking that basement in his name . . . '

Cynthia sat down heavily on the chesterfield, clenching and unclenching her fingers.

'All right, if you want the truth,' she muttered at last. 'Terry Hewlett, in spite of anything he may have said to the contrary, was in love with Sandra. From the moment he met her he invented all kinds of excuses to avoid me — so I decided to teach the pair of them a lesson! I wiped out Sandra and fixed

Terry for the blame. I'd have got away with it, too, if you hadn't been so — so blasted clever! But you'll never find the film that made that illusion! And you'll never find the projector either! They're in the Thames somewhere, deep down in the mud! You can't prove a thing!'

'Our concern,' Garth said quietly, is to prove you murdered Sandra Melbrane, and that we can do to the hilt. As to the basement illusion, the method can be amply demonstrated . . . Now I must repeat my request. Kindly get your outdoor things and let us be on our way.'

Cynthia dragged herself to her feet. Garth looked her dispassionately, then cocked an eye at Whittaker.

'Go with her, sergeant. I'd hate to lose her after the trouble we've been to!'

We do hope that you have enjoyed reading this large print book.

Did you know that all of our titles are available for purchase?

We publish a wide range of high quality large print books including:
Romances, Mysteries, Classics
General Fiction
Non Fiction and Westerns

Special interest titles available in large print are:
The Little Oxford Dictionary
Music Book, Song Book
Hymn Book, Service Book

Also available from us courtesy of Oxford University Press:
Young Readers' Dictionary
(large print edition)
Young Readers' Thesaurus
(large print edition)

For further information or a free brochure, please contact us at:
Ulverscroft Large Print Books Ltd.,
The Green, Bradgate Road, Anstey,
Leicester, LE7 7FU, England.
Tel: (00 44) **0116 236 4325**
Fax: (00 44) **0116 234 0205**

Other titles in the
Linford Mystery Library:

DEATH CALLED AT NIGHT

R. A. Bennett

Jimmy Ellis believes his parents have died in a car crash when as a young boy he is taken to live with relatives in Australia. The years pass happily, then the nightmare comes. Terrifying images flit through his mind in the dark — all through the eyes of a child, a witness to grisly events seventeen years before. He begins to delve into the past, and soon he finds himself on the trail of a double murderer — a murderer who is prepared to kill again.

THE DEAD TALE-TELLERS

John Newton Chance

Jonathan Blake always kept appointments. He had kept many, in all sorts of places, at all sorts of times, but never one like that one he kept in the house in the woods in the fading light of an October day. It seemed a perfect, peaceful place to visit and perhaps take tea and muffins round the fire. But at this appointment his footsteps dragged, for he knew that inside the house the men with whom he had that date were already dead . . .

THREE DAYS TO LIVE

Robert Charles

Mike Harrigan was scar-faced, a drifter, and something of a woman-hater. With his partner Dan Barton he searched the upper reaches of the Rio Negro in the treacherous rain forests of Brazil, lured by a fortune in uncut emeralds. Behind them rode three killers who believed that they had already found the precious stones. And then fate handed Harrigan not emeralds, but the lives of women, three of them nuns, and trapped them all in a vast series of underground caverns.

TURN DOWN AN EMPTY GLASS

Basil Copper

L.A. private detective Mike Faraday is plunged into a bizarre web of Haitian voodoo and murder when the beautiful singer Jenny Lundquist comes to him in fear for her life. Staked out at the lonely Obelisk Point, Mike sees the sinister Legba, the voodoo god of the crossroads, with his cane and straw sack. But Mike discovers that beneath the superstition and an apparently motiveless series of appalling crimes is an ingenious plot — with a multi-million dollar prize.

DEATH IN RETREAT

George Douglas

On a day of retreat for clergy at Overdale House, a resident guest, Martin Pender, is foully murdered. The primary task of the Regional Homicide Squad is to track down the bogus parson who joined the retreat. Subsequent events show that serious political motives lie behind the killing, but the basic lead to it all is missing. Then, three young tearaways corner the killer in the woods, and a chess problem, set out on a board, yields vital evidence.